AF264536

THE MOUNTAIN OF GOD

DAVE BECKER

Published by
Dave Becker

THE MOUNTAIN
OF GOD

THE BIBLE CLAIMS THAT NO ONE CAN SEE GOD AND LIVE. When I was younger, my interpretation of that statement centered around the idea that God wished to remain a mystery. Anyone who dared to steal a glimpse of the Almighty risked death to preserve the secret of his true character and form. I never truly understood the gravity of the concept until I went to Alaska.

My wife and I took an amazing tour of Alaska in the summer of 1992. It's truly a different world up there. Instead of squirrels scurrying around cities as I was accustomed to seeing, caribou wandered the streets. We saw dogsleds, pipelines, glaciers, and our first temperate rainforest. One of the strangest experiences was that it never got dark. The sky would grow dim, and you could see the moon and a few of the brighter stars, but the sky never turned black. As a result, every room we visited was equipped with the thickest curtains I've ever seen, a necessity to create the darkness most of us require to fall asleep at night. And since they had the benefit of twenty-four hours of sunlight, researchers were experimenting with the effect it could have on growing vegetables. At the University of Alaska we saw cabbages as large as watermelons and tomatoes as large as cantaloupes.

But, by far, the most impressive thing was the mountain. Alaska is home to the largest mountain in North America. Most people know it as Mount McKinley, but the natives have called the mountain Denali for thousands of years. That translates as "The Great One," and nothing could be more fitting. Upon arriving at the national park to view the mountain, we were told about the extent of its greatness. While Everest (and more than 180 other peaks) are higher than Denali, they all share the same secret: they're cheaters. They all start at a higher elevation, but from base to peak, they are all smaller than Denali. Denali is the largest mountain on the planet that is situated above sea level. There are several mountains that are larger, but they all begin below sea level, so they can't be completely viewed in their full form. So by default, Denali is the biggest thing on the surface of the earth.

That's impressive enough, but the sight of The Great One is simply stunning. Summers in Alaska are vibrant with color. Dark green trees rise from bright green fields dotted with a rainbow of colored flowers. The lower peaks of the Alaska Range vary from grays to ochers to reds, but Denali never changes. Throughout the year, regardless of the temperature or season, Denali is covered with snow. So in the midst of a warm summer scene stands a solitary figure in stark white, almost as if the mountain was dropped into place from another world.

As we moved toward the interior of the park, we could only see the glistening white base of the mountain. Despite a clear, blue sky, the peak of Denali was shrouded in thick clouds. When we asked when the clouds might dissipate so we could see the entire mountain, we were told a fact that will be etched in my mind for the rest of my life. Denali is so big that it makes its own weather. The Great One is completely unaffected by the environment around it; instead it daily dictates its own weather in defiance to the surrounding climate. The clouds and storms that swirl around its summit rarely disappear. Most people never get to see the peak.

Since we anticipated never being in Alaska again, we asked if there was any possible way to see the top of the mountain. We were told that there was always a slim chance a helicopter could rise above the clouds, but it was often as rare as seeing the peak from the ground. Having never been in a helicopter before, we decided to take the chance. Our pilot was a Vietnam veteran who had flown helicopter missions in the war. That seemed like an ideal navigator to have — until we were up in the air and the pilot began having flashbacks. At least that's what it felt like. Out of nowhere, he would cry out that he spied a grizzly bear or a herd of caribou or some other wildlife, then put the aircraft in a nosedive toward the ground for a closer look. No roller coaster I've ever ridden could compare to the feeling of weightlessness and terror we experienced on that ride. But we did see some magnificent sights as we crossed the surrounding mountains of the Alaska Range toward Denali.

Nearing the base of the mountain, we noticed the pilot wrestling more violently with the control stick. The pilot reiterated that the mountain created its own weather. He further explained that such weather involved hurricane-force winds that would knock the helicopter out of the air and smash it against the ground if we got too close to the mountain. To be safe, we needed to remain 30 miles away from Denali. Thirty miles away from the mountain, and we were still being tossed in the air by the sheer force of The Great One! If by some miracle we managed to survive the torrential winds and venture closer to the mountain, another fate awaited us. Being the biggest thing on the earth, the mountain's gravitational force would eventually suck us into itself and obliterate us against its rocks. We nervously suggested we preferred to avoid any crashing scenario.

The pilot then began to climb through the clouds in an attempt to see the peak of the mountain. The small craft was jostled roughly as it passed through the thickest fog I've ever seen, but we kept rising … 9,000 feet … 10,000 feet … 11,000 feet. Still we could see nothing but dense clouds. The pilot then explained that he could safely go only a thousand more feet; any higher and he would lose control of the helicopter. We held our breath as he thrust the aircraft skyward.

At the last second we burst from the clouds onto a scene that felt like an alternate reality. We were hovering above an ocean of rolling clouds. In every direction, as far as we could see, we were surrounded by a stormy tide of billowing waves. Rising from the center of the surreal sea was the glistening white peak of Denali, sparkling like a diamond in the brilliant sunlight. There we floated, as close as we could possibly get to the biggest thing on earth, a thing so transcendent it defied every environment around it, a thing so massive it created its own weather, a thing so powerful it summoned hurricanes to spin around itself, a thing so magnificent it would destroy anything that dared to inch too close to it. It was beautiful and it was terrifying. It was ethereal and it was overpowering. It was awesome in the most literal sense of the word — daunting, breathtaking, humbling. It was the closest I've ever come to seeing God.

We, of course, took photographs through our narrow helicopter windows, trying to capture the unbelievable majesty of the moment. But we failed. The images were tiny, hazy, and unimpressive. Cameras simply cannot accurately capture the brilliance of a white mountain rising from a white sea of clouds against a radiant light blue sky. And nothing in the photos came close to depicting the awe-inspiring glory of the scene. So when we returned home I tried to recapture it in a five-foot-high oil painting that still hangs in our home today. That same painting is on the cover of this book, and while no part of this story is at all necessary to appreciate or enjoy this book, I'd like to think it adds a little clarity to the grandiose themes that are explored in the following stories. Thanks for reading!

As dreams, as visions longing gaze aloft
Toward peak and steep and crag of splendored bliss,
The whispering giant rose from slumber soft,
The paramount amid the world amiss.
There footed by the billowy sea of cloud,
A subtle halo wrought by holy hands,
He, with almighty imagery endowed,
Adorned in beauty, snow-kissed silence, stands.
The pinnacle of white known but to God,
The burdened buttress fleeting from all sight,
The culminant supreme of lavish, laud
Observant solemnly from lofty height.
Elusive, unengaged in all estatc,
Yet set, the statuesque, the mount, the great.

PROLOGUE

THE MERCILESS SUN BEAT HOT ON A COLD MAN'S HEART. His footsteps slowed and fell into beat with the thunderclaps behind him. Dark clouds hung in the distance, but only blinding dust covered the desert that surrounded him. He longed to see the rain; he longed to feel the rain; but instead he ran. He ran to escape the coming storm, two hundred armed soldiers with an order to execute him. He ran to escape the consequences of his actions, four hundred slaughtered prophets cut down at his word. He ran to escape the crushing doubt, one isolated man abandoned by the God he tried to serve. The scorched earth spread out before him like an endless sea of stone.

Three years ago the heavens had been shut. Not one drop of water, not even dew, had fallen on Israelite soil. By his word it had halted, and by his word the sky again opened, surrendering its storehouses to a dormant land. But there was no time to savor the sweet smell or feel the cool droplets or even enjoy the sight of the parched earth eagerly gulping the rain. Instead his blistered face was pierced by the pelting sand grains of an unwelcoming landscape as he rushed toward death.

He was the last of the prophets of Yahweh, a man of vision, a man of absolutes. In truth, he was a simple peasant, but he held a peculiar position in the social structure of Israel. Priests, kings, and people all sought after the Lord, but he didn't seek. Somehow, he knew. He existed in a different realm, as if composed of matter not wholly temporal, one in the pattern of Moses, the greatest prophet. Transcending the common and touching the supernatural in a unique way, Elijah was, in a sense, God with us. Was.

After three years of drought, Elijah had heard the whisper. It wasn't even a whisper; it was never that real. Every time he sensed the whisper, it was just enough to get his attention, but not nearly enough to convince him it wasn't his own thought. He was certain that the difference between him and every other Israelite was not that he heard the whisper, but that he followed it. And, strangely, others followed him. Was an entire nation simply chasing the delusions of a madman? That was what Mount Carmel was supposed to answer.

From the flattened peak of the mountain Elijah watched dawn break over the Kishon Valley. Thousands of people filled the sloping hillsides beneath him. As he scanned the crowds of doubters, he imagined the drama about to unfold, a play that would pit God against god. A company of eight hundred and fifty prophets opened the spectacle with music and song and dancing and revelry, all to the glory of Ba'al. They quickly moved through prayers and petitions to stunning orations of power and pageantry, legends of beasts brought low, heavenly beings cast down, and a god who once stirred the earth but now seemed impotent. Prophet after prophet cried from the depths of his soul, the lament growing to a desperate frenzy which soon developed into a grisly display of blood, self-immolators attempting to pierce their own souls as only Ba'al once could. With bleeding and weeping and gnashing of teeth, the pitiful performers struggled for hours to elicit a response from their god, but the skies remained silent. The gore continued and several prophets succumbed to death as a horrified crowd stared in disenchanted disgust.

"Enough!" Elijah finally cried. He rose and moved to face a despised and rejected altar of sopping stones. The audience awaited his response to the tumultuous display of the preceding acts. In contrast to the roar of hundreds, one man stood alone in silence. Softly, he asked for fire. A seam ripped open in the scorched sky, and all matter of existence was thrown apart as a fierce tongue of flame spewed from the mouth of God, consuming every holy and unholy thing on that sacred mountain. In the aftermath, the altar embers lay smoldering, the prophets of Ba'al lay dead, and the people of Israel lay on their faces in holy fear, once again baptized by the fire of the living God.

Then fell the rain, and with it a mix of celebration and condemnation. While most of Israel rejoiced at the life-giving rain, a death sentence had been given to Elijah. The blood of the false prophets had fallen on his head, despite the fire, despite the rain. It seemed everyone could only focus on Elijah; no one truly cared about God. So in a final act of desperation, Elijah ran. The man who had shared an unequaled intimacy with God, who had commanded fire from heaven, who had raised the dead — this man now ran for his life. And where was God? Had the Almighty used him to destroy the cult of Ba'al only to watch him, a pawn, be consequently destroyed? The years of miraculous sustenance, the endless conversations, the closeness — all of it was gone. Had it ever been real? As suddenly as the flash of fire had descended, Elijah's assurance had collapsed, and now he ran from death into death, cursing his doubt and cursing his faith.

He ran all day, until the day became darkness, then through the night until dawn. By noon he could run no more. His head swayed and his body slacked, both begging him for rest and nourishment, but the punisher plodded on. He was a day's journey from the nearest town, somewhere in the desert, hardly a sanctuary, but perhaps a fitting sepulcher. His flight had originated out of self-preservation, but his thoughts now turned to self-destruction. In the absence of purpose, his life held no promise. God had abandoned him, and somewhere between the rain and the sand, he had abandoned God. He no longer wanted to see him; he no longer wanted to hear him, he no longer wanted answers. Nothing of the delusional misrepresentation of his past appealed to him anymore. He held neither fight nor faith, nor desire to recapture either. He wanted death.

A solitary shrub appeared like a wraith through the heat and stench of the desert air. His pace had slowed to a stumble, and he began to embrace his inevitable fate. He collapsed in a heap and clutched the base of the shrub. This is true glory, he thought, to choose the circumstance of one's own martyrdom. His eyes slowly closed as the swirling sand dusted his haggard face. To sleep and simply cease was now his final wish. The tired seer in desperate slumber conceded victory to a vanished God, and softly breathed, "Let me die."

Elijah awoke to the touch of a stranger and the smell of burning wood. The cool of the evening was warmed by the light of a small fire near his bush. Cautiously, he moved toward the inviting flames, pausing to imbibe the entire scene — the red night sky, the glowing mountains, the air of serenity. Something heavenly had descended here, he mused, and he soon perceived a small cask of water by the fire. He sat deathly still for a moment, fiercely struggling to ignore the too-obvious wooden vessel. In time he succumbed, and to his astonishment, his lips met the sweetest water he had ever tasted. It seemed to flow with its own pulse; it almost breathed. He reclined with an ecstatic gasp, filled with wonder, filled with life. Emotions began clamoring in his skull, elations began hammering at his heart, and for a brief second, he saw God.

No, a man, a crouched figure, resolutely defining a distance between himself and the prophet, but undeniably staring at him. Elijah searched the silhouetted face. There was an eerie alienness in its form, but whether it was simply a stranger or something more he could not determine. Something certainly contradicted the presence of this being, yet nothing negated its humanity. It was no specter, for he had felt its touch. It was no man he had ever viewed before. No matter, it was not God.

So the Almighty had refused the request of the still-living Elijah. Life was, after all, the breath of God, and Elijah's life was perhaps his God's most telling drama. For a time, his life had seemed to be the very breath of God. Were he never to speak another holy word, it could never negate the power of the reality he once walked. Other than Moses, no other prophet had spoken the truths or performed the marvelous wonders of Elijah. If life itself be damned, his never would be! But as surely as God lived, who had denied him his presence, Elijah could no longer live with the torturous strain of providence. To live and forever search is not to live, the prophet thought; the weight of existence is more than enough. At this point, to die would be his greatest gain.

The stranger silently stared. Elijah returned his gaze as he reached into the coals for a bit of food, a freshly baked cake of bread, clearly prepared by the mysterious guest. Elijah paused and pondered, who was the guest here? Had this man come upon him, or had Elijah wandered onto his land? Ah, there was the searching again. Stop searching for meaning everywhere, Elijah scolded himself. Here was a man and nothing more. Elijah struggled to banish the suspicions from his mind, but suddenly his thoughts became more physical as the taste of the cake swelled in his mouth. He looked in astonishment at the bread in his hand. The flaky, white pastry tasted like wafers made with honey. He clenched his eyes shut in disbelief, but the cry of his senses betrayed his desire to despise. At once he knew what had entered him, a grace that had not fallen on the tongue of an Israelite for over five hundred years: manna.

He tossed the bread aside, fell to the ground, and covered his face. He had not asked for any of this. Why was God toying with him? Must a man be cursed to ask the unanswerable, to seek the invisible, to eternally scream into the emptiness of heaven, and know that no answer will ever come? He refused to return to his past position, the man of God without God. No one could be burdened with that, and he could endure no more. I am no longer a prophet, he told himself; I am merely a man like any other man. He began to dream as the night chilled his weary soul.

Dawn's sun pierced the morning, and the stranger's touch again roused Elijah to face a new day. Elijah sat upright and reflected on the past forty-eight hours, marveling at the spell that could effortlessly drive a man from zealot to apostate to nihilist. He surveyed the lifeless desert around him. There were legends that the area had once been fertile. Everything exists only to die, he thought, shielding his face from the punishing sunlight. The former prophet had already weathered one drought; he wasn't about to sustain another.

"You should eat. The journey will be too much for you," the stranger finally spoke.

Elijah had forgotten he wasn't alone.

"Who are you?" he demanded.

"A humble servant of God like you," the man replied enigmatically.

"A servant of God," Elijah mused. "I envy your simple, blind faith. That type of faith I never knew when I was the prophet of God."

The stranger smiled in a way that conveyed both sympathy and contempt.

"When did you cease to be the prophet of God?" he gently asked.

Elijah stammered for a moment, then curtailed the rage that nearly erupted from his mouth.

"How dare you...," he warned, motioning a shaky finger toward his assailant. Then he paused to compose himself.

"You have no idea what I've seen. You can't know, because I don't even know anymore! I've commanded drought and deluge! I've been fed by birds and sustained by a handful of flour! I've raised dead children up from the earth and called fire down from heaven! I have heard the Lord's voice and felt his touch more than anyone else alive! I have also persevered through long seasons of doubt and silence, and the only thing that held me together was the unwavering belief that his presence would one day return.

"But I'm tired. I'm tired of wrapping all of my hopes in the occasional glimpses of a God that ignores me most of the time. I've been orphaned and left for dead. If I return home the queen will have my head and the king will have my hands for trophies. I will forever be remembered as the prophet who raised his sword to the throat of Ba'al only to find myself destroyed. All this I could bear, but one thing has crushed my soul. God is gone again. He doesn't speak. He doesn't move. He doesn't touch. No light can shine from a darkened prophet, and I've had enough. He has abandoned me for the last time."

Elijah sank to the ground in exasperation. Only the subtle sounds of the tiny fire crackled through the silent desert landscape. The stranger continued to stare at Elijah.

Then, inexplicably, the man rose. "You should eat," he reiterated. "The journey will be too much for you." With that he turned and departed.

Elijah watched in relief as the stranger strode away, displacing his melancholy long enough to shout, "What journey?"

No answer came.

Eat indeed, Elijah scoffed; I want to die. Hours seemed to pass, how many the prophet could not discern, but it was long enough for his visitor to completely vanish, leaving Elijah altogether alone with only his shrub, his fire and his jug. He began to weep softly, mourning the life he still clutched but wished he could release, and the God he had lost. Somewhere, deep inside his heart, he still wanted both.

He snatched the open container of water, drank, and spat in horror. The water was — wine! Elijah leaped to his feet and began spinning, circling, searching for explanations. No water for miles, but he had tasted the sweetest drink last night. How had it become wine? He remembered the cake — manna — the bread of heaven! At once, it all became clear. This man was sent from God, sent to save Elijah in his hour of weakness. He began to follow the soft impressions in the sand, quite unconsciously at first, but was soon chasing the mysterious footprints. His heart began beating faster as his pace accelerated to a run. Maybe God had not abandoned him!

Then the footprints ended. Elijah stood, dumbfounded, staring across the vast plain of unmarked earth. He moved slowly, steadily seeking a clue to the man's end or exit. No sign of life, no motion in the hills could be perceived. He stopped, and a small chill shot through his nerves. This was no man; this was a holy messenger from God. And his message had been simple: eat.

Elijah stumbled back to the shrub and snatched one of the manna cakes from the ground. He paced around the fire as he ate, staring into the flames and fighting to make sense of the entire encounter. His understanding of angels was sparse. To him they were bearers of flaming swords, conveyors of death, hypnotic instruments of God's wrath on earth. But this man had done very little and said even less. A fire and some food, he thought as he gulped more of the wine, and a strange statement about a journey. Elijah wasn't on a journey; he was on a flight.

As he downed the last of his provisions he reflected on everything that had failed to summon his God. Prayer had yielded nothing. Fasting had yielded nothing. Self-denial had yielded nothing. Desperation had yielded nothing. His flight into the desert had yielded nothing. Despite his experiences, all that remained before him was a tiny burning fire.

Suddenly, he noticed the fire, the fire which had burned since his first encounter with the angel, the fire which had continually burned for the past two days, the fire which now burned, leaving no ash, consuming no bit of the wood below. And a name immediately came to his mind: Moses. No prophet had ever equaled Moses; he knew God like no one else. His own face had glowed with the glory of the Lord. He spoke with God face to face. That, that is what Elijah wanted — no mystery, no guesswork, no distance. He lifted his head, gazed to the south, and one object consumed his thoughts, one particular mountain that rose above the Sinai Desert. With a newfound passion, Elijah ran. He ran with zest; he ran with zeal; he ran to see his God, all the while repeating one name: Moses, Moses, Moses.

Elijah entered the dark cave slowly, pausing to remove his sandals and shake off the dust of two hundred desert miles. He brushed his weathered hands reverently over the rough walls. Here was a temple that paled Solomon's, a holy haven that all of nature fell to worship. Power seemed to pulse from its cracks. He traced the perimeter of the tiny hollow, gently sliding his fingers over the black stones, lost in the otherworldliness of the place. It was here that, for Elijah, history had been split.

He settled onto the cold floor and stared at the red rays of the setting sun that filtered through the cave entrance. Elijah had come to the mountain of God. This was the mountain where Moses worshipped before a bush that burned but was not consumed. This was the mountain where Moses received the tablets of stone written by the finger of God. This was the mountain where Moses was baptized with a privileged fire, the first man to hear the holy name of the Lord. This was the mountain where God chose a friend, and repeatedly drew the man to himself as never before. That was what Elijah desired; what he longed to see, hear, and feel. He huddled against the soundless stone wall, closed his eyes, and muttered to himself.

"Moses saw God here."

For a moment his head reeled with all the thoughts and wishes he had ever dared to dream. He opened his eyes and sighed in sorrow. There was no trembling earth, no blinding light, no burning fire, no visible God. His stomach tightened as his logical mind tried once again to suffocate his faith, but he had come too far. Here was the spot, and here he would wait until death for God to return. Surely the Lord would honor this ground, if not for his servant Elijah, certainly for his friend Moses. Tears began to trickle down the cheeks of the prophet who felt he had fallen from grace. Tomorrow he may embrace his God; tonight he embraced what he could. A stone served as his pillow and the cold, dirt floor chilled his bones as he curled into a ball and began to drift to sleep. He rolled over and watched the daylight slowly turn to darkness.

HE ROLLED OVER AND WATCHED THE DAYLIGHT SLOWLY TURN TO DARKNESS. The tent flap fluttered in the early morning breeze. Moses clutched the folds of his robe and trembled. He knew what was coming, or more accurately, who was coming. The rest of the camp had no idea.

Dark, spotty clouds crawled across the gray sky. Moses followed their movement from the entrance to his tent. He watched them melt into the heavy fog that had enveloped the peak of Mount Sinai. Flashes of lightning sliced through the clouds. The glimmering mass swirled slowly around the rocky crest like the luminous haze of a dim lamp. Moses thought back to the first time he had set foot on the mountain. A burning bush and a barely audible voice had completely terrified him. The plagues that had leveled the most powerful nation in the world had horrified everyone. Whatever was about to happen was going to be much worse.

He knew the sun was just beginning its ascent as he moved through the camp in the early morning dew, but he couldn't see it. It was completely concealed behind the thickening clouds. The only light in the sky was the constant flashing that came from the mountaintop. By the time he reached the edge of the camp, the cloud that encircled the mountain had grown blacker, denser, and more ominous. Thunder began to roll down the mountaintop.

"Is he up there?"

Moses turned to find his brother, Aaron, by his side. Behind him was a trembling group of eleven elders, cowering a safe distance from the two leaders.

"Not yet," Moses answered. "He's waiting for us."

Aaron lifted a shaky finger toward the rumbling mountain. "He wants the elders to approach that?"

"Not the elders, everyone," Moses said with a quaver in his voice, "and that's nothing compared to what's coming."

Aaron gulped and motioned for the elders to gather the tribes. When they were beyond earshot he asked, "I thought he was taking us to a land of milk and honey."

Moses shook his head. "That was always an incidental. We were never bound for the promised land. We were bound for here, bound for this mountain, bound for an encounter with the God of the Ages."

He could feel a chill of horror shudder through his entire body as the first few Israelites tentatively crept from their darkened tents. Within an hour, the entire assembly was nervously gazing at the clouded peak of the quaking mountain. Moses took a deep breath, then stepped toward the base of Mount Sinai. From the youngest babe to the oldest sage, the entire nation of Israel followed its leader to the smoking beast before them. The thunder swelled to a constant roar and the lightning became sharper and more frequent. Moses stumbled slightly as the ground began to shift. He moved to the front of the assembly, paused for a second, then raised his staff over his head.

A piercing shrill resounded like a trumpet blast of immense proportion. Moses staggered in the blaring sound and the stiffening wind that seemed to portend a coming storm. The Israelites shriveled in horror, but Moses continued to face the incessant noise. A spear of lightning suddenly shot down the rocky clefts. Everyone, including Moses, screamed. The trumpet grew louder and louder as most people fell on their faces around the foot of the mountain. Lightning continued to flash toward the crowd through fog and cloud and smoke. The earth beneath them reverberated to the peals of thunder atop the mountain. Moses began to weep, too fearful to request an exemption from this experience.

An explosion erupted from the crest of the mountain like a volcano, and ash and smoke settled all around the quivering crowd. The heavens stood agape, and fire burst from a hole in the clouds, plummeting to the shuddering rocks below. The tremulous landscape threw everyone violently to the ground. The people clapped their hands over their ears, shielding them from the thunderous blaze and the blaring horns which clamored louder with every second. They turned to one another and screamed, unable to capture any view through the thick smoke and eclipsing tumult.

Finally, Moses managed to struggle to his feet,

and through all the noise, called out to God. The mountain quieted for a moment, then a deafening voice boomed from on high, sending a rushing tempest that knocked Moses onto his back, bristled over the shivering crowd, and flattened the tents behind them. The sound was unbearably loud, drowning the roaring thunder and blaring trumpet that continued to drone under what could only be compared to a mix of crashing ocean waves and screaming army hordes. Moses gripped his head, feeling as if every cell in his body was about to explode. Amid the piercing blast were the constant flares of fire and lightning. Rocks and ash continued to rain over the assembly.

Again the landscape stilled, just long enough for Moses to lift his head. Then the entire mountain erupted in fire and the earsplitting voice returned. Smoke swirled around the scene. The earth convulsed under the weight of the presence that seemed to crush every molecule of surrounding matter. Moses barely discerned a word through the tumultuous storm. Ten times God thundered from the mountaintop. Every time, the force of his voice physically thrust the thousands of Israelites away from the mountain, sliding them along the shuddering rocks through explosions of light and sound.

Eventually a single beam of sunlight pierced through the thick clouds and hit Moses full in the face. His ears were ringing so loudly he could hear nothing. The ground never stopped quaking, but it calmed enough for him to stand shakily. Aaron emerged from the huddled mass of terrified people still trembling flat against the desert floor. He clutched his brother and the two men stared up at the glowing spire of now molten rocks.

"Why is he so angry at us?" Aaron asked fearfully.

Moses shook his head. "He's not angry. He's revealing himself to us, his true self."

"His true self is terrifying."

"I know," Moses said with the faintest hint of a smile," but he is what he is."

Aaron glanced at the rest of the Israelites, their faces pressed to the ground, and wondered aloud, "What happened to our savior, the God who rescued us from Egypt and led us to safety in a pillar of cloud and fire?"

"He's still up there," Moses mused. "He's just a lot bigger."

"He's too big," Aaron protested. He turned to face his brothers and sisters and added, "He's obviously too big for them."

Moses squinted through the smoke that covered his people. Tiny pieces of stone skittered over the trembling desert surface. No one dared to lift their heads or speak a word. Maybe Aaron was right. Maybe all of this was too much for them.

"Go warn the people not to come near the mountain so they remain safe."

Aaron scoffed, "None of them feel safe, and none of them have the slightest desire to approach this mountain."

Moses sighed. "Go tell them."

Aaron left Moses to deliver the message, then returned with a response from the huddled masses.

"Not only do they want to flee this mountain,

they never want to hear God's voice again. If you want to face this being, so be it, but they refuse. They'll listen to you, but they want nothing to do with him."

A violent rumble rolled from the shrouded peak down the rough faces of the mountain like a trembling tear. Moses stepped forward and yelled over the people.

"Don't be afraid! Your God wants you to be his sacred treasure. Don't you want to be embraced by the greatest love in all the world?"

A muffled but resounding response met his ears.

"No. We will only listen to you, not him."

Moses opened his mouth to speak, but could find no words. Only choking tears filled his throat. He gazed over the trembling tribes as if peering at them from a mountaintop. If they only knew, he thought, how often he had dreamed of uniting these people with the God of the Universe. Ever since the burning bush he had waited for this day, and here they lay, unyielding and unwilling.

Moses wiped his face and gazed up at the swirling storm clouds. Fire and lightning continued to flash over the mountain, filling his heart with dread while strangely compelling him to reach the summit. The landscape continued to quake, and as Aaron and the Israelites remained on their faces, Moses stepped toward the smoldering hillside. Alone and afraid, he climbed the shaky rocks.

ALONE AND AFRAID, HE CLIMBED THE SHAKY ROCKS. The old man stopped at the edge of an overlook and scanned the area. He was exhausted from a brutal three-day journey and an equally brutal three-day battle within his tortured mind. Thoughts of obedience and defiance clashed in sparks of rational and irrational arguments. His head hurt, his feet ached, and his eyes were bleary with sweat and sand, but he swore he had seen them again.

Abraham glanced back at his servants and his son. The three young men were laughing as they gave the donkey a drink of water. In the middle of a parched desert, Isaac was trying to give life in the midst of death. If only he knew what awaited him at the top of the mountain. If only he knew how wracked with guilt and doubt his faithful father had become. If only he knew how harsh and uncaring his God had grown. All Abraham could do now was hope for a sign, and he thought he had seen one. But the surrounding sand silently sifted over the desolate landscape.

"Where is your wife Sarah?"

Abraham spun around to find the three men he

believed he had spied earlier.

Only the tallest man ever spoke to him. He carried himself with the air of royalty, the ruler of a distant clan or kingdom, one not of this world. The pelt of a white ram covered his shoulders and draped down his back, and the head of the ram served as a crown. Gleaming, ebony horns curled around the man's ears, framing his dark, weathered face like a warrior's helmet. A large scar shaped like a teardrop dipped from his left eye.

"Where is your wife?" the ruler repeated.

"She wants no part of this," Abraham answered, eyeing the two servants who stood behind their master.

They never spoke. From the first time he had met them to now, he had never heard them utter a sound. They simply carried out the will of the king, even if it was a death sentence. Abraham shuddered at the memory of a decimated valley.

"I want no part of this," he added tentatively.

"And yet here you are," the man observed through squinting eyes.

"At your behest," Abraham almost shouted. He glanced back at his son briefly, realizing the boy could neither see nor hear him from his position.

"I promised I'd return to you," the man reminded him.

"Yes, a promise I thought was supposed to validate the boy's miraculous birth, not demand his murder!"

"Sacrifice," the ruler corrected.

"I've seen your idea of sacrifice. I've smelled the burning sulfur and seen the smoke of a thousand deaths. You sweep away the innocent with the guilty!"

An eerie smile crept over the face of the mysterious man. "You accuse me of things you've never seen."

"I asked if you would spare the city for ten righteous people!"

"But you never asked me to save Lot."

Abraham took a step backward. The man was right.

"I was too afraid," Abraham confessed.

"Afraid of my response?"

"No, afraid of your lack of response."

The man opened his hands toward Abraham and said, "So instead you never asked, and now you will never know what became of your nephew."

Abraham closed his eyes. He had spent many years and many expeditions trying to find any trace of his relatives. Most days he assumed Lot and his family had perished in the burning of Sodom, but now and again something stirred within him that compelled him to look. There would always be a part of him that hoped his nephew had been spared.

"And what of my son?" he finally asked, returning to the conversation. "What of Isaac? Is he another innocent that must die?"

The man shook his head. "You still ask the wrong questions."

"Spare my son," Abraham blurted as tears filled his eyes. "Please, for his mother's sake, for your servant's sake, please, save my son."

"Perhaps you love your son too much."

"Is that a crime?" Abraham cried.

"Perhaps you love your son more than me," the mysterious man added.

"Right now I do," Abraham groaned.

The man turned and nodded toward his servants. The two men descended the mountain trail and soon disappeared.

"Oh, not again," Abraham sobbed.

"It's getting late," the ruler said, staring toward the west. "You and Isaac must finish the climb."

With that the man set off in a different direction, leaving Abraham to weep alone. The reddening clouds flowed like blood across the sky. From his ledge, the desert haze seemed to Abraham to condense like the smoke from a raging furnace. He shuddered. All he had wanted for the past two days was for God to change his mind. When he finally appeared, Abraham was convinced for a second that he had. But no, like his cold disappearance before the destruction of Sodom, he had spoken with Abraham like a friend and then disregarded the deepest desire of his friend's heart.

Abraham wiped his face. Maybe Sarah was right. Maybe this God demanded too much. The old man squinted across the barren desert. But God had given so much, he reminded himself. Promises, provisions, position, purpose … and a son. None of it would have been possible without the hand of God. And now it seemed it was all being taken away. Sarah had told him to simply refuse God's request, but Abraham was convinced that doing so would result in all their deaths. He could sacrifice one of them or all of them. Sarah didn't want to live without Isaac. Abraham wasn't sure he could live without him either, but something compelled him to obey. Maybe it was the fact that everything had come from God, so giving it back shouldn't be an unreasonable request. Maybe it was the hope that this step of faith, like every other, would result in a reality much greater than anything he had experienced before. Maybe it was just fear.

He composed himself, resolved himself to the horrible task again, and returned to his son and his servants. The sound of laughter pierced his heart and he closed his eyes to offer one more silent prayer to save his son. Silence was all he received in return. The Lord had spoken. Isaac was already dead.

"Isaac," he stammered, fighting hard to sound strong, "grab the wood for the sacrifice."

While his son collected the wood, Abraham turned to his servants. "Stay here with the donkey. The boy and I will make our sacrifice at the top of the mountain;" he paused to choke down his tears before finishing, "and then we will both return."

He tied the wood on Isaac's back, grabbed a knife and a torch, and began climbing to the peak of the mountain. The setting sun bathed the pale stones in a disturbing red glow. Abraham imagined he was scaling a heap of bones covered in blood. If God didn't change his mind, that would soon be exactly what Abraham was doing — sloshing through his own son's blood.

"Father," Isaac spoke, "aren't we missing something?"

Abraham closed his eyes. This was the question

he had been dreading since they left their home.

"Where's the lamb for the sacrifice?"

Abraham took a deep breath but refused to look at his son.

"It's somewhere up there," the old man lied. "God is going to provide the lamb."

The idea seemed to make sense to Isaac, which wrenched Abraham's heart even more because none of this made any sense to him. He thought his God was different from all the stories he had heard as a child. He thought his God was good and kind. He thought his God cared. If he had known he was following a blood-thirsty monster maybe he never would have left Ur. And then he never would have found the promised land. And then Isaac never would have been born. And there would be no legacy and no blessing to the world.

Abraham violently shook his head, trying to rattle those ridiculous thoughts from his brain. He had repeated those words of God to himself for so long that they had become a part of his very soul, despite the fact that he had no idea what they meant anymore. How could his tiny family ever become a nation? How could that nation change the world? How could any of it happen if he killed the promised child?

They reached the broad crest of the mountain just as the last moments of daylight turned the rocks to gold. Abraham stumbled into a clearing among a thick collection of thorn bushes. Without a word, he turned and cut the sticks from Isaac's back. The father and son arranged the wood in silence, beginning with two parallel rows. Abraham paused, remembering the first time the Lord had appeared to him. He searched the area in earnest, hoping the floating fiery pot would appear again. Only the lonely call of a solitary vulture echoed overhead. The old man shook his head and began placing the remaining sticks across the base of the altar as a platform. Isaac stared at his father in confusion.

"That's a strange altar, Father," he commented. "It looks more like a bed."

Abraham stood shakily and reached for the twine that had held the wood against his son's back.

"And I still don't see a lamb...."

Abraham seized his son before the boy could finish his sentence. Despite the old man's age, he quickly overpowered the unsuspecting lad, pinning him to the ground under the full weight of his sobbing body. Within seconds, Isaac was bound.

"What are you doing?" the boy screamed repeatedly.

Abraham couldn't speak. He couldn't think. His actions were almost involuntary as he flipped his son onto the broad altar. Any thought, any pause would jeopardize the sacrifice. He had spent three days of utter torture, but somewhere during the climb he had made the decision to follow God's order, his own soul be damned. Maybe his life would finally find peace, maybe he would be left in eternal anguish, but he couldn't fight the tormenting fear that shrouded his heart. God only seemed to care about one thing, and he wouldn't leave Abraham alone until the man did it.

Abraham pressed his hand hard against Isaac as

the boy continued to writhe and scream. The old man reached for the knife. Isaac stilled for a second, his eyes wide with terror.

"Father, no, no, no, no, no!"

Abraham pressed the knife to Isaac's throat.

"Abraham!"

The voice was immediately recognizable. It was God. Abraham searched frantically for the mysterious king he had spoken to just moments ago. In the dim twilight he finally spied the man's headdress through the twisted branches of the surrounding shrubs. He took a few staggering steps toward the figure and gasped.

Gleaming, ebony horns curled around the thick, white wool of an enormous ram's head. The animal was entangled in the sharp briars. Large spikes pierced its body in numerous places, dotting the animal with blood stains. A thin wreath of thorns twisted around the animal's head like a crown. For a moment, Abraham thought the ram was weeping, then he realized a familiar-looking scar shaped like a teardrop adorned the animal's left eye.

"I promised I'd return to you," the ram spoke.

"I don't understand," Abraham whispered. "I thought you wanted Isaac."

"I never wanted Isaac; I wanted you to experience resurrection."

Abraham glanced at his son, still bound and crying on the altar, and said, "There must have been another way."

"It's impossible to experience the joy of resurrection without first feeling the deep despair of death."

Tears streamed down the ram's face. Abraham untied his son and gripped the boy in his trembling arms. Neither one could speak.

The ram continued, "Because you feared me enough to follow, and I loved your family enough to save you, a new sacrifice must be made."

Abraham approached the animal. He held the knife against God's throat. Suddenly he was gripped with a new fear, one that made him think that killing this ram would be even harder than killing his own son. The sun vanished beneath the horizon, causing the red-stained ram skin to gleam like a golden statue.

THE IMAGE OF GOD

THE SUN VANISHED BENEATH THE HO-
RIZON, CAUSING THE RED-STAINED RAM
SKIN TO GLEAM LIKE A GOLDEN STATUE.
Aaron stared at the curtains that covered the tabernacle. Smoke still crept from the concealed area
and curled around the drapery. A burning smell
covered the area. Aaron closed his eyes and took a
deep breath of the acrid air. It had been almost a
year since he had smelled the same awful odor.

Just three hours ago, the corpses of his two oldest sons, Nadab and Abihu, had been dragged
from the tabernacle and burned on the garbage
heap outside the camp. No funeral, no burial, no
mourning — Aaron had even been forbidden by
his younger brother to show any sign of grief. His
greatest loss as a father and he couldn't even cry
for his boys. The only solace he could find was hidden in the very area where his sons had met their
fate. He pushed the curtains aside and stepped into
the sanctuary.

The smell was even stronger in the enclosed holy
place. Wisps of smoke mixed with the shadow of
clouds that continually filled the area. Aaron approached the golden altar and slowly wrapped his

hand around one of the horns that jutted from its corner. This was the last place his sons had stood alive. A tear fell from the old man's face and sizzled upon striking the still-smoking surface of the altar. The twisted pieces of a slaughtered goat, the substitutionary sin offering for the entire camp, still covered the surface of the altar. Here, hidden from everyone in the camp including Moses, he could finally weep. He stepped around the altar and gripped another horn, resting the full weight of his frame against the structure. His hands began to tremble. Aaron squeezed the horns of the altar as if he were staring into the face of a small bull. It was like a sacrifice. It was like his worst sacrifice.

Nine months ago Aaron was standing at the base of a violent mountain covered in cloud and fire. Their God had seemed to swallow his servant Moses and left the new nation to their own devices. As the temporary leader — perhaps the new permanent leader — Aaron needed to maintain order. The people of Israel had seen enough of God to know they didn't want to deal with him at all, but they had also experienced enough to know they owed their lives to him. It was up to Aaron to figure out how to reconnect the people with their God.

So he borrowed an image the people understood, one they were more comfortable approaching and praising. He fashioned a small, golden calf from the people's jewelry, a symbol of power and divinity known throughout the Semitic region. It wasn't an idol; it was never meant to be an idol. In Aaron's mind, he was simply providing a more palatable image of God. For a people who had been traumatized by thunder and fire, it was a welcome substitution. And with that calf Aaron had declared a festival of worship to the God who had rescued his people from bondage.

But God rejected his worship, just like he had rejected Aaron as leader in favor of Moses. To this day Aaron still didn't understand God's objection. After thousands of Israelites were slaughtered for Aaron's sin, the high priest had simply chosen to push the incident aside without an explanation and follow the new laws as best he could. Now his sons were dead, cut down by the same God for the same sin. All they wanted to do was worship God. Moved by their genuine love and adoration for the Lord, Nadab and Abihu had filled their censers with incense and presented an offering of fire. In response, God answered them with fire, blasting them with a funnel of flames that burst from the ark of the covenant in the Holy of Holies. Two young men were killed because they loved God. And once again, Aaron didn't understand.

He released the horns and dropped his hands to his side. What he wanted more than anything else was an answer. Why had God taken his sons? He paused, then wept again. The Lord had erupted in anger and then fallen silent. No answer was coming. Aaron stepped toward the ornate curtain that concealed the holiest place in the tabernacle. A few charred remains clung to the tattered hole where the fire had pierced the fabric before piercing his sons. Even if the Lord were to answer him, he probably wouldn't survive.

"Aaron," came a soft whisper like a breath of

wind through the cloud, barely audible, scarcely real.

The priest began to tremble. Suddenly he didn't want an answer. He didn't want an encounter with the being who had annihilated his children in an instant.

"Aaron."

The fog that filled the room thickened and swirled. Aaron knew it was senseless to run. No one could escape the supreme spiritual being of the universe. His heart felt like it was bulging from his chest. The curtains wafted in the swelling breeze. Aaron had a sense of what was on the other side of the curtain. He had spied a glimpse of God once before, almost one year ago, for the briefest of seconds. That momentary peek was enough to terrify him and convince him he never wanted to see God again. But the voice kept beckoning, and the wind kept swirling, and an invisible force kept pulling him toward the Holy of Holies. The priest finally succumbed and passed through the veil to behold an even more astounding sight.

The floor of the tabernacle was transformed into a sparkling, blue surface that reflected everything around it. Two enormous feet were barely discernible through the raging flames that surrounded them. Whatever being was standing before Aaron extended far above the clouds that covered the tabernacle. Aaron fell to his knees in tears.

"You haven't eaten anything," the voice murmured.

"How can I eat, my Lord? My sons are gone, dead at your hands."

The flames that filled the room swelled, terrifying Aaron with the dread that he was about to be incinerated. But instead the room grew softly warmer. Something like an embrace surrounded the elderly priest.

"They just wanted to worship you," Aaron sobbed.

"No, they wanted to honor themselves," the voice corrected.

"No! No!" Aaron thrashed his arms against the clouds, fighting to shrug off the feeling that gripped his body. "That's the same lie that was told about me! It wasn't true with the calf and it isn't true now! We were worshipping you!"

"Is it worship to disregard the wishes of your king?"

"It was love," Aaron explained. "Sometimes we do stupid things for love. Have you no mercy?"

"Mercy?"

For the first time the room began to feel hot. Beads of sweat formed on Aaron's face.

"You're still speaking," God thundered. "That's mercy. Your sons were allowed to pursue their ritual to its completion while they ignored my pleadings with them to stop. That's mercy. The entire nation of Israel still exists despite their grumblings against me and sometimes downright loathing of me. That's mercy."

Aaron pressed his face against the reflective floor. The mysterious stone surface felt cool against his hot flesh.

"Tell me this," the Lord continued, "where's the mercy for me? First I'm denied the honor I deserve, then I'm denied the right to punish the dishonor. Am I a stone statue that's simply supposed to silently accept any gift that's offered to me?"

"We're not perfect," Aaron lifted his head and whimpered. "We're frail and flawed creatures who simply want to offer you our sacrifice."

"You ignore my commands and insist on offering your own chosen gift. How is that a sacrifice at all?"

Aaron protested, "What's so awful about a child giving an imperfect gift to his father?"

"The fact that you believe I want a gift."

The priest flopped on the floor in exasperation.

"I don't understand," he moaned.

"What can you offer me that I don't already have?"

"Nothing," Aaron answered after a long pause.

"So any sacrifice that you bring originally comes from me. You're simply presenting to me what I gave to you, correct?"

Aaron nodded silently.

"It isn't a gift at all. The entire scheme is a set-up that exists for one purpose: to spend time with you. I want to connect with you — your heart, your mind, your soul. It's not about you giving me a thing; it's about you giving me yourself. It's realizing you have nothing to offer me and saying with awe and wonder, 'Daddy, help me make something for you.' That is the innocence and intimacy I crave. And that's the one thing you people never want to give me. You'll blindly slaughter animals for days, set fires that burn for weeks, sing songs and recite prayers that drone on with such volume and duration that they eventually drown out the sound of my voice in your ears. You'll do anything to keep from facing me, and you convince yourselves that you're doing it because you love me. But you truly want nothing to do with me."

"If we're all such disappointments to you then why did my sons have to die? What was so much worse about what they did?"

The flames that surrounded the Lord raged hotter and brighter. Aaron shielded his eyes and coughed violently as the searing heat burned his throat.

"You and your sons have been charged with distinguishing between the sacred and the secular. Your sons, more than anyone else, were chosen to teach my people how to follow my laws and how to connect with me. If they refused to take that task seriously, they could only mislead and hurt the people who follow them."

Aaron disagreed, but he was too afraid to argue. He wrapped his arms around his head and sobbed into the sleeves of his robe. After several minutes a chill crept over the old man's body. Aaron lifted his head and noticed that the sapphire floor had evaporated into the desert dust. The chamber was silent and the flames were gone. Even the cloud had vacated the tabernacle. God was gone.

The high priest shuffled out of the holy place and returned to the golden altar. He stood for a long time and stared at the slaughtered goat. According to the law he was supposed to eat the animal as an act of worship. But he had no appetite and no desire for worship. His heart still felt the hollow pangs of grief for his sons, and his mind still harbored a

fierce anger for the God who had taken them, terrified him, and then vanished. There was nothing
left inside him to worship.

He snatched one of the torches and struck the
carcass on the altar. The animal burst into flames.
Aaron looked around the sanctuary in fear. He
fully expected God to strike him down as well for
his defiance. But no punishment came. The curtains that shielded the room didn't move. No sound
but the crackling fire could be heard. Aaron closed
his eyes and moved to the entrance. He placed his
hand against the heavy curtain and struggled to
still his breathing. Eventually he dared to exit the
sanctuary. The cold night air sliced at his lungs like
a knife as he listened fearfully for any sound.

THE COLD NIGHT AIR SLICED AT HIS LUNGS LIKE A KNIFE AS HE LISTENED FEARFULLY FOR ANY SOUND. The wind swept gently through the reeds as Jacob paced along the bank of the stream. He searched the darkness of the opposite shore, pondering the safety of all he held dear. Everything he owned, everything he loved was now separated from him. Long ago he had schemed for these things. Now, terrified he could lose it all, he finally understood the price of his success. His destiny was seeded across the water like a frail desert weed. As darkness consumed the bitter night, bleak dreams gave way to black despair. The cloudy shadows swallowed the concealed tents of his divided family, and his mind wandered past each of his sons and wives as if visiting them for the last time.

Tomorrow's dawn would herald the arrival of four hundred enemy men led in weaponed procession by the man who had sworn to kill Jacob twenty years earlier: his brother, Esau. Esau was a man of strength. He was the firstborn, larger, rugged, and eternally more powerful than Jacob. Esau was a man of confidence. Having had his fortunes and blessings ruthlessly ripped from his hands, he had resigned himself to his place but somehow never lost the aura that was rightfully his. His was the leadership; his was the future; his was the life, eternally more powerful than Jacob. Esau was a man of success. Jacob may have duped his father into proclaiming him a great nation, but it was Esau who realized that destiny. Long before Jacob might ever dream of possessing any land, chiefs of many territories had arisen throughout the hills of Seir, and the roots of a wealthy trade kingdom were spreading like weeds ready to devour a deceiver. All of his calculated fraudulence and dishonest gain had failed; through all of Jacob's striving to steal it away, Esau had been blessed, and that unpronounced blessing was rolling forth in justice and vengeance to punish sins of the past, and to offer a younger brother's clan as an obliterating sacrifice to a God who apparently had changed his mind. Jacob wiped cold tears from his eyes and shuddered. He could see the man approaching, enormous, violent, god-like, eternally more powerful than Jacob.

The man was approaching. Jacob shook himself from his sleepy reflections and noticed a large figure tracing the ford against a dark landscape. The moonlight revealed the anger in his gait, the force of his stride, the beastliness of his movements, and Jacob whimpered as he recognized the unforgettable coarse hair covering the man's broad shoulders and chiseled arms. This was Esau. If needed, he could summon his kingdom to utterly destroy his brother, but Jacob knew it wasn't needed. Esau was very capable of slaying Jacob's entire camp alone. Jacob crouched among the taller grasses and watched nervously as the hunter-warrior strode nearer. After twenty years he was still impressive. His hulking frame moved very determinedly along the shore, and the crushing sounds of the brittle weeds beneath his weight were beginning to chant a sinister eulogy for his pitiful brother.

Apparently the bribe hadn't been enough. Before dusk, Jacob had instructed nine of his servants to drive nearly six hundred animals toward the outskirts of Esau's camp. The gift was intended to precede Jacob and ideally buy his brother's favor. No doubt Esau had hamstrung the animals and murdered his servants. Now as Jacob shrunk deep into the shadows of the earth which would inevitably soon drink his blood, his entire body began to tremble, much like the seizure he had caused in his father when his duplicity had been revealed so many years ago. He pressed his beard into the sod, almost unable to discern the hunter's silhouette as it searched the area for sign or scurry. Esau's form was soon hidden from Jacob's eyes by the same vegetation which increasingly crackled with his coming, louder and louder, nearer and nearer. It was completely hopeless. Esau was a predator. Scent or sound or sight would eventually betray his hidden prey, and even if Jacob could miraculously evade his brother's keen perception in the darkness, the daylight would certainly surrender him at dawn. Tonight was his last; Esau was relentless; Jacob was dead. Silently, shudderingly, Jacob began to whisper a prayer.

"Remember what you promised me, that you

would always protect my children and never leave me."

He clenched his eyes and tried to imagine a staircase that stretched into the night sky. Glowing warriors descended the shimmering stairs, passing the victors that climbed to heaven. The cries of the celestial army roared overhead like the crashing of ocean waves.

"At least let Joseph live," Jacob softly pleaded.

He stopped. All noise had eerily ceased. Opening his eyes, he saw a monstrous sea of dark clouds sweeping over the moon, covering the entire scene with a black shroud as if hiding the next Cain from God. Jacob mustered enough courage to raise his head. Through the weeds he could see the glowing outline of his brother only a few yards away. The monster was staring intently across the stream. Jacob followed his gaze. The tents! He had attempted to conceal them, but in his haste, had his efforts only served to mark them? Were they even visible in the pitch of this night? He strained his eyes, darting back and forth between his family and his executioner. The hunter nodded and stepped into the water.

"Esau!" Jacob rose from the reeds and screamed, "Leave my family alone!"

The dark figure paused and turned toward the sound, then with the swiftness of a wild beast, he charged toward Jacob. Instinctively, Jacob ran away from the shore, wanting only to lead Esau away from his wives and children. After a few strides, he was caught from behind in the iron grip of his brother's woolly arms. Jacob struggled against the clamp, kicking and beating against his foe. In an unbelievable moment of strength, he broke free, whirled around, and pounded his fist into his brother's jaw. God had promised him a destiny, and he may die fighting on this field, but he would die fighting.

Esau reclaimed his hold, and again Jacob wriggled free and struck. Repeatedly, Esau clutched his younger brother with all of his might, and each time the clutch was broken, until Jacob's hands were covered with bloody bits of his brother's face, but he fought on. Jacob kept darting through the darkness, evading those clasping hands, and attacking with flailing fists. Minutes soon turned to hours, and both men groaned with exhaustion, but neither would surrender.

As the battle raged throughout the night, Jacob began to wonder why Esau had yet to strike him. Perhaps his prayer had been answered, or perhaps he had summoned an even greater power. More than merely saving, his God was delivering his enemy into his hands. Filled with fury, Jacob lashed out like the beast he believed his brother to be, knocking Esau to the ground, only to be knocked down himself in Esau's powerful grapple. Clawing, clubbing, crying, the twins wrestled against one another, one to hold, one to break.

Finally, Esau threw the full weight of his massive body atop Jacob, pinned him against the hard soil, wrapped one of his great arms around his smaller brother's body, and jammed one finger into the socket of Jacob's hip. A piercing howl echoed throughout the valley. Searing pain like the blades of a thousand daggers shot through his entire body, and Jacob collapsed, nearly lifeless. He remained under the heaviness of his brother in quiet stillness for over an hour.

As the clouds slowly rolled west, gradually revealing the first light of dawn, Esau slowly rose from his brother. Jacob, recovering from his delirium but still in excruciating agony, rolled onto his back and groaned, "What did you d...?"

He froze mid-sentence. His eyes grew wide and wild. Standing before him, lighted by the unrisen sun, was a man bloody and swollen, almost beyond recognition. Almost. His matted beard clung to the tattered, leather garments of Esau. The scent of sweat and game pouring from the heaving, weary combatant was the stench of Esau. But Jacob glared into a face which horrifyingly was not the face of Esau. This man had contrived the cruelest impersonation, stolen his brother's best clothes, and wrapped his arms in goat hair. Jacob was staring at his own face.

"Odd," the other Jacob panted, "I've never experienced a hug that hurt so much."

He turned to leave, but Jacob writhed on the ground, stretched forward, and grasped the man's heel. "Who are you?" he begged.

"Let me go," the strange twin huffed. "It's daybreak."

"But please ... what's your name?"

The man jerked his foot from Jacob's hand, and spoke very directly, very deeply, straight to the core of Jacob's soul, "What's your name?"

"Jacob," came the meek reply.

He grabbed Jacob's shoulders in his bruised arms and lifted him to his feet. Through the discolored pockets surrounding his piercing but familiar eyes, blackened and torn by Jacob's fists, Jacob could sense a warmth and acceptance that defied reason, and a sense of peace enveloped him which momentarily eased the pain in his hip. He could see tears mixing with the grime and grooves on his twin's battered face, and sweat that mixed with drops of blood. Jacob had nearly killed himself. The man embraced Jacob strongly and began to weep strongly. Jacob became limp in his arms.

"O Jacob, Jacob. Maybe … maybe you are my deceiver, but no more. Your name will no longer be Jacob, but now you will be the Princess of God, Israel."

The stranger released Jacob and stepped away. As the sun peeked above the mountains its rays blinded Jacob's eyes. He covered his face and pleaded once more to know the name of his opponent.

"Why do you want to know my name?" the man tenderly inquired with outstretched arms, and in a blaze of dazzling white light, vanished. Jacob rolled onto his back and panted heavily, gazing up at the clouds while he struggled to make sense of the entire experience. He had a new name, a new injury, and all the same problems. After spending a night with the divine, nothing had really changed.

After hours of mental anguish, he finally tried to stand. The same searing pain erupted from his hip and shot through his entire body. He held his breath and counted the seconds until it subsided enough for him to open his eyes. The rising sun bathed the field around him in golden light. His shallow breaths punctuated the dull throbbing that lingered. Squinting across the river he could see the first signs of life emerging from the tents. His family was still alive. That was something. Maybe that was everything.

He shifted his weight and tried the aching leg. Whatever the stranger had done to him, his leg would never be the same. Perhaps that was the point. He wasn't a new man; he was a damaged man. For a moment, he wondered if somehow he had forfeited something profound out of irrational fear, like selling his soul for a bowl of stew. The light of a new day warmed his face, and he softly prayed that it held some promise for him. With agonizing effort, Jacob, Israel, began limping toward the river to join his family. Steam rose like smoke from the broad, grassy plain.

STEAM ROSE LIKE SMOKE FROM THE BROAD, GRASSY PLAIN. The massive gold statue of the king loomed over the swelling flames of the waiting furnace. Gleaming reflections billowed over the face of the idol while thick smoke curled around its feet. Azariah stared at the haunting form, mesmerized by how lifelike it appeared as the shifting highlights slid over its surface. Its eyes seemed to glow with rage.

Hananiah and Mishael walked ahead of Azariah, their hands bound with thick ropes that also wrapped around their entire torsos. Their sentence had been delivered so quickly and so fiercely that the customary protocols of execution had been abandoned. All three men still wore their royal garments, turbans, and shoes. They had been hastily and ridiculously bound like animals, and were now being marched to their death. In the sight of the king and his court, they were to be burned alive before the very image they refused to worship.

Azariah could feel the heat of the intensified furnace as they approached. In his anger, King Nebuchadnezzar had ordered the furnace to be stoked seven times hotter to obliterate the obstinate Jews as quickly as possible. As his feet stepped onto the stone platform, Azariah could feel the heat begin to melt the soles of his shoes. The largest guards he had ever seen in all of Babylon coiled the same ropes around the length of his legs. With a scream, the guards lifted Azariah and his friends above their heads, preparing to toss them into the furnace. But before they could complete the act, they were immediately engulfed in flames from the raging inferno beneath them. The guards' howls of adrenaline turned to shrieks of agony as the men were consumed in seconds. Azariah slipped through the disintegrating arms of the immolated guard and plummeted through the flames to the stone floor of the furnace. He landed with a bone-shattering thud that paralyzed his body and his lungs. Gasping in the scorching heat, he thrashed on the floor like a dying fish.

When he regained his breath, he lifted his right hand to his chest. The heat around him was almost unbearable, and his entire body ached from the fall. Suddenly he realized his hand had been freed. He sat up painfully. All of his bonds were gone, as if burned by the surrounding flames, but his clothes were completely unscorched. He stood up slowly and gazed at his feet. Fire licked around his shoes, almost shrouding his feet from view, but while he could definitely feel the intense heat, he was not being burned or harmed.

He looked for his friends. Hananiah and Mishael stood nearby in a similar state of amazement. Hananiah extended his hand with a small flicker of flame dancing in his palm. Walls of fire surrounded the three men like showers of hot rain, radiating all around them with simultaneous sensations of warmth and coolness.

"Why are we not burning?" Azariah finally asked.

"Perhaps God will save us from this," Hananiah offered.

All three men caught their breath at the same time, remembering the bold statement they had made to the king as a defense. The words had spilled from their mouths without thought or preparation, almost as if someone else was speaking through them. Just then, the color of the entire furnace changed from red to blue, and the flames calmed to pillars as tall as a man. The heat disappeared, and the three friends found themselves in the middle of what looked like an army of blue allies. The golden idol above them stepped into the flames and began shrinking until a solitary burning figure stood in the center of the furnace, glowing white hot with eyes of blazing red. The fiery idol approached them, and instinctively the three men fell to their faces in reverence.

"Don't be afraid," the being said, his voice sounding like a thousand shouting soldiers. "Stand and face me."

Azariah rose shakily and was the first who dared to speak. "Who are you?"

The terrifying figure almost seemed to smile.

"I am the first and last of all things, and in my hands I hold both life and death." After a pause, he added, "In my hands, I hold your life and death."

At the sound of the voice, Azariah and his friends collapsed to the floor. The mysterious man reached

out and touched them, and they found themselves
back on their feet.

"You claimed that I would save you, but you
didn't expect me to appear?"

Azariah averted his eyes and thought about the
question for a long time before speaking. "We
believed you could save us, but we believed you
weren't obligated to save us. We were unsure if you
wanted to save us, and if you did appear, we never
dreamed it would be like this."

The burning figure laughed, and the flames all
around them seemed to dance to the rhythm of
his joy.

"Oh, the eternal doubt of my children is both
comical and heartbreaking. For a thousand years
your people have honored me with their lips while
systematically ignoring me. Sometimes it seems
you desire anything but me."

"Sometimes our desires get muddled with our
thoughts," Azariah offered. "It's hard for us mor-
tals to tell the difference between our dreams
and reality, and we're terrified to choose or act
wrongly"

"Why can't dreams and reality be the same
thing?"

Azariah glanced at his friends. None of them
had an answer for that. When he turned back to
face the divine being, the flaming man had transformed back into a golden statue that gleamed in
the firelight.

"Very few people are punished for what they do,"
the golden man continued. "Most are punished for
what they do not do. Your prophets have constant-

ly reminded you of all my laws. Not one of them is particularly more important than another, just as not one of your options is particularly better than another. You have at any time at your disposal a multitude of best choices. The greatest sin is not choosing incorrectly; it's not choosing."

Azariah stared at the man in confused disbelief. He could not even form the words to construct a question to communicate his lack of understanding.

The brilliant form gathered an armful of flames, which transformed into tiny, dancing figures in his hands. Twirling and swaying, leaping and bowing, the dancers appeared fixated on their God, oblivious to everything else around them, and almost careless in their movements.

"The birds of the air and the flowers of the field don't anguish over their choices. They simply be. You can spend your life wondering what God wants you to do, or you can spend your life being with God. When you remember the greatest reality, suddenly your dreams seem the most logical choices."

The mysterious visitor gazed lovingly at the tiny dancers and added, "It's the freest and easiest way to live."

The flame figures vanished into the air, and the divine being returned his gaze to the three young men in the furnace. His piercing, red eyes seemed to burn through their souls as his body began to grow.

"I know you're weak. You're allowed to doubt. You're even allowed to fail. But you're not allowed to forget. That's what has separated my children from the rest of humanity since the dawn of time. Those who remember have the confidence to hold a truth in their hands for a thousand years, and against all reason and evidence, never let that truth go. That kind of faith frees a creature to simply be."

He extended his glowing arms, and the three men felt themselves drawn to the immense body of the living statue. A warm sensation enveloped them and spread throughout their bodies as the golden man wrapped his heavy arms around them in a fiery embrace. Then he pressed his scorching lips against Azariah's face in a burning kiss.

"Remember," he whispered in Azariah's ear.

The burning man's aura intensified, growing to a blinding glare. Azariah and his friends once again collapsed onto the floor and shielded their faces. The huge statue stepped out of the furnace and took its place again. The deafening sound of a thousand rushing winds filled their ears, and when the light and the sound dissipated, the three men found themselves surrounded by the same yellow flames they had originally experienced upon being cast into the furnace. The intense heat returned, almost unbearable, but the fire still failed to burn a single hair on their bodies.

Above them, the sound of King Nebuchadnezzar's voice could be heard bellowing orders to pull Azariah, Hananiah, and Mishael from the furnace. Metal spears were lowered into the flames, and although they began to glow red hot from the raging inferno, even the molten metal did not scald the hands of the three young men. When Azariah placed his feet on the platform overlooking the furnace, he stared for a moment at the torturous flames that should have consumed him, then lifted his face to the golden statue. Once again it stood, lifeless, under the cloudy sky. The overcast heavens cast a shadow over Azariah's face that both cooled and refreshed him. A single drop of water fell on his lips like the morning dew.

A SINGLE DROP OF WATER FELL ON HIS LIPS LIKE THE MORNING DEW. Samuel licked the sweet moisture and opened his eyes. It was still dark. The faint flickering of the sanctuary lamp provided the only light, casting soft shadows on the walls of Samuel's tiny room. The boy gazed groggily at the earth-colored walls. He thought he had heard something, but the entire tabernacle was deathly quiet.

Samuel adjusted his tunic and lay back down on his mat. He gazed at the colorful robe that hung over his bed, an annual gift from his mother. The fabric almost looked alive in the shifting firelight of the small room. Most nights he imagined the robe was his mother and would talk with her. The only home he could ever remember was the tabernacle, and while he understood it was a great honor and privilege to live there, it was a lonely existence for a boy. His surrogate parent was the old, blind priest Eli, whose history as a father was abysmal. Eli's sons were the worst criminals in Israel; Samuel constantly heard complaints about them from everyone who visited the tabernacle. But Eli never took any action against them, much like he never really interacted with Samuel. The boy could count on one hand the number of meaningful conversations he had had with his guardian.

Which is why Samuel leaped with excitement when he heard the call of his name. Or at least he thought he had heard it. He paused for a second, then rushed to Eli's room, hoping the old priest needed to tell him something very important in the middle of the night. But Eli's room was pitch black, and the priest was dead asleep.

Samuel shook the old man and said, "Here I am. You called me."

Eli snorted and sputtered before answering hoarsely, "I didn't call you. Go back to bed."

Samuel sadly plodded back to his silent room and dropped onto his mat. A solitary tear dribbled down his cheek. He so wanted to have a talk — with anyone. The flickering candlelight cast taunting shadows around his tiny room. He stared at the colorful garment that hung above him for what seemed like hours. Finally he stood and approached the robe nervously. He slowly took the sleeves and wrapped them around himself. Pressing his face into the fabric, he began to weep. He imagined he could hear his mother softly whispering his name as she stroked him gently. He sniffled and paused. No, it was truly his name he heard. It was Eli again.

He ran to the priest's room again to find the same scene, only this time Eli was snoring like an ox. Samuel shook him and repeated, "I'm here. You called me again."

Eli again denied calling the boy, but Samuel suggested that perhaps he had cried out in his sleep, just hoping to prolong the conversation, any conversation.

Eli brushed him off dismissively, groaning, "No, no, no. Just go back to bed and stop waking me."

Samuel stormed out of the room, smacked his fist against the walls, and threw himself onto the ground in disgust. Now he was angry. His teacher was either being deliberately heartless or he had lost his mind, but Samuel knew he had called. Eli wasn't ever playful, but this seemed like a sick game designed to torment Samuel. He tried to calm himself, but the thought of the old priest taunting him kept burning in his mind like a smoldering sacrifice. How was this entertaining for him? Did he really hate Samuel that much? All the nagging fears of abandonment and rejection began to flood his mind. The room seemed to grow darker and colder, and then he heard his name again, louder and clearer than ever before.

"I know you called me," he bellowed as he stomped into Eli's dark room.

The old man stirred and eventually lifted himself onto one elbow. Samuel stood defiantly, arms crossed, daring the priest to deny it a third time. Eli rubbed his face and paused for a long moment. Then he raised his head and seemed to stare at the black ceiling in silence as if he had suddenly remembered some powerful secret from long ago. He motioned for the boy to approach.

"Come sit next to me," he gently said.

Samuel complied, and Eli placed his leathery hand on the boy's face. Samuel closed his eyes. It was the first time he had been touched in months.

"Return to your room. If you hear your name again, simply say, 'Speak; your servant is listening.' I don't know what will happen, but don't come back here. I'm not the one calling your name."

Samuel began to tremble, and nervously asked, "Who is it?"

Eli shook his head and answered, "I don't want to say, and if I'm right, I'm terrified of what he wants to say."

Samuel could feel the terror in Eli's touch. He slunk back to his room and crawled onto his bed. Staring at the lights dancing across the ceiling, he couldn't imagine who was calling him if it wasn't Eli. And if the old priest was scared to his bones, what did that mean for Samuel? The anticipation was excruciating, and just when he thought it might never happen again, he heard his name a fourth time. The walls of his room quaked at the sound of the call. Samuel swallowed hard and mumbled the words Eli had given him.

"Speak; your servant is listening."

The flame of the lamp began to grow slowly. The boy clutched his blanket and covered his face. Eventually, the room became so warm that Samuel had to emerge from his covering. When he did, the lamp flame immediately flew out of the room like a bird. Samuel leaped from his bed and followed. The light bounced off the walls and darted into one of the darkened rooms. Samuel chased the light throughout the tabernacle, ducking into various nooks and excitedly trying to catch it. It finally shot behind the heavy curtain that protected the central sanctuary. The boy knew he was forbidden to enter the space; everyone was. But the lure of the light was overpowering. He slowly crept behind the drapery.

He stared in awe at the walls of the unfamiliar room. It seemed otherworldly. A golden glow danced over the walls like a rolling ocean. Everything felt alive with motion. Bright, colorful lights like sparkling gems swirled through the air. The dirt floor glimmered like jasper.

The voice grew louder and clearer. "Samuel."

"Yes," the boy answered nervously.

"I am the great scale that weighs the deeds of the earth."

Samuel didn't understand, and he still could not see anyone in his room. He gazed at his upside-down image in the translucent floor. Standing before him within the reflection was a fiery figure, but when he lifted his head, he could only see the golden ark in the middle of the room.

"I have come down to judge Eli and his family. I'm about to do something that will make everyone in Israel's ears burn and their hearts sink."

The more the voice spoke, the more Samuel's ears burned and his heart sank. Each syllable grew louder than the previous one until he could feel the words reverberating in his small chest. The boy remained speechless, paralyzed with fear.

"I warned Eli that his family would be forever cursed if he continued to ignore the sins of his sons. Those scoundrels honor me with their lips only; their hearts are far from me. They make a mockery of my laws and dishonor my covenant, so I will remove my covenant from them. Eli and his sons will die on the same day, and all Israel will suffer for their disobedience because no one will be able to offer a sacrifice for their atonement."

Samuel shuddered and gazed wildly around the space. This prophecy seemed to indicate that the nation would be decimated and their house of worship would be destroyed. The boy had spent his entire life living and ministering within the tabernacle, serving the God of the universe with particularly prescribed prayers and rituals. What would become of him and his people if their entire religion was stripped away?

"Fear not, Samuel," the bodiless voice assured him. "The day is coming when all sacrifices will cease. They were always a temporary shadow of a greater truth. I never wanted bleeding and burning animals; I only ever wanted your hearts. Obedience has always been better than sacrifice. You of all people must learn this."

"I don't understand," the boy finally spoke.

"Understanding will come in time," the voice said more gently.

Samuel felt a peace return to the room, and what seemed like a heavy weight rested on his right shoulder. It was almost as if a giant had placed his hand on the lad. The force seemed to move the boy out of the holiest place. Samuel walked slowly back to his room with his invisible guide.

"As for you, you will lead my people. But like a hen longs to gather her unwilling chicks beneath her wings, you will grieve and weep and suffer for all of Israel because they will ultimately reject you as they have always done to me."

"So I will always be alone?" Samuel softly inquired.

"You'll never be alone," the voice answered. "You will always have me."

Samuel entered his room and shakily approached his robe hanging on the wall. The voice was gone, and the boy felt frightfully alone again. He pressed his face against his colorful garment. All the years of loneliness he had endured collided with all the years of loneliness that were to come, and for one brief moment he sobbed into the only bosom he could fashion. The room grew cold and silent. Samuel stepped back and gazed around the dark room, wondering if the experience had been real. The lamp lights provided the only movement on the lifeless walls. He brushed the tears from his eyes and stared at the flames.

HE BRUSHED THE TEARS FROM HIS EYES AND STARED AT THE FLAMES. Jerusalem was burning, and it was all his fault. David stood on the portico of the palace and surveyed the damage. Thousands had to be dead. He scanned the various sectors of the city, unconsciously counting the toll, then caught himself and shuddered. Counting is what had spawned all of this destruction.

The elders of Israel knelt behind the king clad in sackcloth, partly as a show of solidarity, partly by order of the king. David wore the same, hoping against hope that earnest mourning would stem the scourge. He grimaced at the stench of decaying flesh and sulfur that filled his nostrils. It had only been a few hours; how could Israel sustain three days of this?

Suddenly the sky ripped open and a massive, fiery being descended through the clouds. Everyone behind David fled in terror, leaving the king to face whatever new hellish horror was coming alone. The flaming warrior drew a huge sword from his side and leveled it at the city. David trembled, believing this assassin was coming for him. Against the burning backdrop of this new curse, the silhouette of a shadowy figure slowly rose from the stone steps, backlit by the glow of the smoldering city. It was the prophet Gad, the man David trusted more than anyone else, but also the man who had delivered the news that this carnage was coming. David wiped his face and braced himself for more bad news. Gad turned for a moment and took in the grisly scene.

"You chose this," the prophet finally said.

"I was hoping the mercy of God would cushion his wrath, but it turns out it's a terrifying thing to fall into the hands of the living God."

Gad nodded in agreement. "And it's about to grow more terrifying."

David closed his eyes and held his breath.

"He wants to talk to you."

The king gulped, then took a step forward.

"And tell twelve of your officials to each bring a stone for an altar," Gad added.

David and his men followed the prophet down the steps from the palace and slowly climbed up the rise to the highest point in Jerusalem where a broad threshing area filled the top of a flattened hill. The plot of land was owned by Araunah, one of the last remaining members of the oldest family that had ruled Jerusalem before David conquered the city and made it his capital. Araunah was usually one of the most confident leaders of the community, but he was currently facedown in the dirt, quivering in fear. David glanced up to see the celestial figure towering over them, his body blinding like the fiery sun, his sword hovering just over their heads. Despite his own fear, the weight of the day was suddenly causing David to burn with anger.

"There was a poor man who lived in Jerusalem," David shouted. "He owned a small ewe lamb that he treated like a daughter. It ate from his table, it drank from his cup, and it slept in his arms. One day, the wealthiest man in the city paid a visit to the poor man and demanded the ewe lamb for himself. When the poor man refused, the wealthy man stole the lamb. Hearing what had happened, the king ordered that the ewe lamb be killed as punishment."

The flaming figure burned brighter and hotter as if seething with an increased rage.

"You try to distort my words against me, but you speak a greater truth."

"Why are you punishing these innocent people?" David continued to scream. "They're only sheep! I'm their shepherd! I'm the one who ordered the census! Pour out your wrath on me and my family, but stop this plague now! It's unjust!"

"Unjust?" the giant bellowed, driving every person to the ground. "You would lecture me on justice — you, who actually murdered a poor family's lamb?"

"And you didn't punish me then, either! You killed my baby and cursed my family, but you never punished me! You always strike the weakest people!"

David began to weep. He curled up on the ground like a child, muttering to himself just above a whisper.

"You always punish the wrong people."

"Look at yourself," the fiery being said sadly. "How can you say you haven't been punished?

From the day I plucked you out of obscurity your life has been filled with trouble."

"But I'm still here. A life of trouble has to be better than a life extinguished."

"Constant suffering is better than what awaits you after death?"

"I don't know," David sobbed, realizing he had no idea what happened after death. "I don't know. I just know this can't be right. What about forgiveness?"

"Forgiveness requires sacrifice."

"What is the value of a slaughtered animal on a pile of ashes to you?" David demanded.

The elders behind him took a few cautious steps backward, the altar stones still in their hands.

"Your desire is a broken spirit and a contrite heart," the king mumbled to himself.

"My desire is for you. The question is what do you desire? Whatever you treasure, your heart follows."

David shook his head in exasperation.

"I just want all of this to end."

He glanced up at the terrifying being. He thought he saw the faintest trace of a smile shining from the blazing face.

"Just build the altar," the colossus ordered.

David rose slowly and approached Araunah. The owner of the land was still trembling on the ground. The king grabbed Araunah's shoulders and lifted him to his feet.

"I want to buy this land so I can build an altar and stop this plague."

Araunah shook violently in David's arms. His

eyes darted between the fiery being and the king's face.

"Just take it. Take the oxen; take the wood; take it all."

"No," David insisted, "a sacrifice that cost me nothing is no sacrifice at all."

He pulled a bag of gold from his tattered garb and placed it in Araunah's quavering hands. The trembling man fell to his knees.

"May your God accept you," he whispered, "for all of our souls."

David collected the stones from his elders and stacked them in a small pile directly under the flaming sword. As he finished assembling the tiny altar, a vague figure approached him from the city smoke. It was a man carrying a lamb. David glanced at the fiery figure towering above him, then turned to face the man. It was Jonathan.

The king gasped, then embraced his lost friend and began to weep. It had been so many years since the prince had died, but David had mourned for him every day. Deep in his heart, he knew this couldn't be real, but he held tightly to his friend, relishing every second of the moment as long as it lasted. Finally the two men stepped away from one another, and David gazed into the eyes of Jonathan, which looked exactly as they had the last time they had been together.

"I told you you would be king," Jonathan said with a smile, "and the greatest one Israel has ever seen."

David lowered his head and whispered, "I'm not great, especially without you. I've failed this nation so many times, and now it's burning because of me."

"You've always doubted yourself and your calling. That's what made you the perfect leader."

Jonathan handed the lamb to his friend.

"It still does," he added.

David continued to cry as his closest friend silently walked away. When he had disappeared back into the haze, another figure emerged. This man was clad in the armor of a decorated soldier. When he grew close enough, David recognized the face of Abner.

"My ghosts are coming to visit me," the king sighed happily. "Hello, old friend."

Abner bowed before the ruler.

"You're the one who made me king," David confessed.

"Not so," Abner answered. "God made you king, and it took me too many years to accept that. My actions were far too little and far too late."

The late general placed a silver coin in David's hand. The king examined the coin closely. One side depicted a lion and lamb lying on the ground together under the shield of David. The other side bore an image of the king's face. It was a coin that had never been minted by David's order.

"Where did you get this?" the king asked.

"It's for your offering," Abner said and then turned away.

David placed the lamb and the coin onto the small altar, and wiped the tears from his face. When he rose, he saw a third figure striding from the darkness. Against the reddened flames and smoke, distinctive curls of long hair waved over the broad shoulders of a confident man. Even as a silhouette, David immediately knew the man. The king ran forward, grabbed his son in a tight embrace, and began kissing him.

"O Absalom, my son," David wept, "if only I had died instead of you."

"Father," Absalom answered, "don't call me your son. I am unworthy of such a title and such kindness."

"No, no, no," the heartbroken father pleaded, "I never stopped loving you, and I never stopped looking for you, and I never stopped missing you."

"How could you forgive me?" Absalom demanded. "I thought I would make a better king than you, but I was wrong. You are the true king of Israel, the chosen one of God."

David heaved against the strong chest of his departed son. He could barely stand. All the anguish and loss collapsed on him like a giant weight. He refused to release his son because he knew as soon as he did, the vision would walk away. Even if he wasn't truly Absalom, he wanted nothing more than to have a form of his son remain with him forever.

"Don't leave me," David insisted. "Don't ever leave me."

"I never have," a voice answered from above his head.

David glanced up at the fiery figure, still extending his sword overhead. When he lowered his head, Absalom was gone. He looked at the altar to find the lamb and coin also vanished. Again he stood alone before the terrifying destroyer.

"I'm not punishing anyone," the Lord explained. "I'm preparing a sacrifice, and by its very nature, sacrifice hurts. It hurts everyone involved, but none more than me."

"Your preparation feels angry, and your anger is terrifying," David said softly.

"I know. It has to be so. But my anger is never directed at you or your people. It is always directed at the chasm between us. That is what I always attack to bring you back. But it will always be dreadful and it will always be painful. That's what makes it real."

David nodded silently and placed his hand on the head of the larger ox. He took a deep breath and whispered a wordless prayer. For a moment, everything around him vanished. The terrifying giant, the trembling elders, the traumatized family, the transcendent visions, the very threshing floor — all of it melted into a calm haze, and for the first time in a long time, David felt the arms of God close tightly around him. The king's tears dotted the animal's head, and he wondered if maybe his closest times with God had always been when he felt furthest from him.

He opened his eyes and prepared to slaughter the ox. With knife in hand, he paused and glanced at the ground beneath him. A single, red seed of wheat lay at his right foot. He stooped and lifted the seed to his face. The red spot was a drop of blood from the quivering ox. He rolled the seed between his fingers, feeling the rough husk slowly fray and fall.

HE ROLLED THE SEED BETWEEN HIS FINGERS, FEELING THE ROUGH HUSK SLOWLY FRAY AND FALL. The stone pit where he was hiding was dark and musty and never intended for threshing. It was a winepress. But Gideon was afraid, and it had been three days since his family had eaten. He just needed to get enough kernels of wheat to bake a single loaf of bread.

A faint sound outside made him freeze in terror. He had been working all morning to collect a tiny amount of wheat for flour; he couldn't afford to lose it again to the Midianite raiders. After several minutes of absolute stillness, he exhaled slowly and returned to his tedious task.

"Mighty warrior!" a voice called from outside the pit.

Gideon slowly rose to his feet and peered above the rim of the winepress. A stranger was sitting on a rock under an oak tree, holding a long staff. Gideon squinted at the shaded man. He didn't look like a Midianite, but he also didn't look like an Israelite.

"Are you a friend or foe?" Gideon called.

"Neither," the stranger answered. "I've simply come to see the mighty warrior that God has chosen."

Gideon looked around, assuming there was someone else that fit that description.

"Mighty warrior? I'm the least important member of the weakest family of the smallest tribe in all of Israel. I think you have the wrong man."

"Are you saying God has chosen in error?"

Gideon dropped his head. He crawled out of his pit and approached the man.

"I'm saying you are in error. God hasn't chosen me because God hasn't chosen anyone. He's abandoned us."

The stranger whistled softly, his breath mixing with the faintest breeze that rolled delicately over the fields.

"That's a bold accusation for the least of the weakest of the smallest to make."

Gideon could feel his face reddening, and his voice grew louder.

"I grew up with stories of wonders and miracles, parted seas and swallowing chasms, tales of a God who decimated the most powerful nation in the world to rescue his chosen people from slavery. Look around us! Where is he? That God is gone."

The unfamiliar man slowly turned his head in every direction, then finally answered, "I'm not sure what you would expect to see, but it seems to me an invisible God would look exactly like this, whether he were here or not."

"Where are his deeds?" Gideon demanded. "Where are his signs? Where is our salvation? For seven years, the Midianites have raided our land, destroyed our crops, slaughtered our livestock, and terrorized our people. All of Israel has become ravaged and impoverished. Again I ask, where is our salvation?"

"Salvation is here," the stranger said with a crooked smile, extending his staff toward Gideon. "You will rescue Israel from the grip of the Midianites."

Gideon laughed, "You're delusional. Plus that doesn't answer the question. Where is God?"

"He never left you. And now I'm sending you. I'm sending you like a sheep among wolves to destroy Midian once and for all."

Gideon pointed at the winepress and shouted, "I can't even feed my family! How am I going to rescue a nation?"

"With the strength you have," the man mused coyly, twisting his staff in his hand, "and the strength I have."

Gideon gazed at the spinning staff, half expecting it to transform into a snake, or make water gush from the ground. A kernel of hope began to sprout in his heart.

"If what you say is true, and if you truly are who I think you are, give me a sign."

With a smile of satisfaction, the stranger asked, "How much wheat have you threshed in your little hole?"

"Enough for one loaf of bread," Gideon answered with embarrassment.

"Bake that for me."

Gideon stared at the man with suspicion for a long time before turning back toward the winepress. With a newfound excitement, he jumped into the winepress, collected the flour, and rushed into his house. In addition to the bread, he prepared a tiny goat he had been saving until it had grown. Within a few minutes, he returned with a small basket of rare meat and flatbread along with a pot of broth.

The stranger rose and motioned toward his former seat.

"Place the meat and bread on the rock, then pour the broth over it."

Gideon did as he was commanded. The stranger approached Gideon and thrust his staff into the hard dirt, nearly missing Gideon's foot.

"So you desire to see the signs and wonders of your God? That is what you require to believe again?"

Gideon swallowed hard and nodded nervously.

"You just prepared all the food you had saved for your family for me. You have nothing left. Clearly you believe something, or you've betrayed your entire family."

Gideon shrugged. The man sighed, then stretched his staff toward the rock and touched the tip to the food. Fire burst from the spot and immediately consumed everything on the rock. Gideon fell backward in fear and awe.

The stranger stepped onto the rock and stood in the middle of the fire. The flames climbed around his body, burning away his clothes and transforming him into a glowing bronze being. Gideon wanted to scream in terror, but no sound would come from his mouth.

"Relax and breathe," the flaming man said, sensing Gideon's terror, "you're not going to die. On the contrary, your life will bring deliverance for millions now and millions to come."

Gideon unconsciously exhaled. He could feel his heart pumping so hard he believed it might burst from his chest.

"You say your God has abandoned you. You say he has failed to act and has vanished from your lives. What you say is not true, so you will be the one to show all of Israel just how present and powerful the Lord can be."

The being's voice grew louder with every word, eventually ringing in Gideon's ears to the point where he could barely discern what was being said. The more the man spoke, the fainter Gideon became, and he soon feared he would collapse into complete unconsciousness.

"Go in strength, go in courage, and go in the certainty that I will save Israel through you," the man bellowed.

With that, he shot into the heavens in a pillar of fire. Gideon gasped and fell facedown into the sharp grass. After a few moments, he slowly crawled to the rock and placed his hand against it. It was still warm, and almost throbbed with the pulses of an earthly object that had been blessed with a divine visitation. He almost wished the ordeal had not been real because he had no idea how to begin the deliverance of his nation.

Lifting his fingers to his nose, he noticed they smelled like incense. He pressed his hand against his robe, and his fingers formed a strange pattern on the fabric. It almost looked like a priestly ephod. This was all too much to absorb, and certainly more than he could understand, but a small part of him wished he could devise some way for the experience to remain. His fingers continued to tingle for a long time, but eventually every sign that he had seen a miracle was gone. All that remained was the same quiet scene and his memories. Deep in thought, he carefully rubbed his blistered hand over his head.

DEEP IN THOUGHT, HE CAREFULLY RUBBED HIS BLISTERED HAND OVER HIS HEAD. A thin stubble was all that remained of his former mane. His fingers slid down his sweaty forehead and gently traced the rims around his eyes. He wanted to cry, but no tears could form from the scarred edges of his gouged sockets. The dank air of the prison cell filled his lungs, the smell of blood and death surrounded him, and the chilling shroud of absolute blackness was the only thing he would ever see.

He grabbed the millstone and returned to his incessant grinding. His fingers had become chipped and raw from hours of scraping one rock over another, preparing grain for his sworn enemies. Being their prisoner was bad enough, but the thought of helping to feed the people he hated most in all the earth was demoralizing.

"I ruined everything," he whispered to no one.

"How did you do that?" the voice of a child answered.

Samson's entire body tensed.

"I ... I thought I was alone. When did you get here?"

"I've always been here," the boy said coyly.

"Where did the Philistines capture you?"

"I'm no one's captive."

Samson was confused. He assumed the child was also confused. Why would a little boy chained to a prison wall not believe he was a prisoner?

"I'm not chained like you," the boy responded to Samson's unspoken thought. "Now how do you believe you ruined everything?"

Samson sighed, "I broke my vow. Now I'm being punished along with the rest of my people."

"Nonsense," the boy cried. "Why would your god punish you for such a small thing?"

"It's no small thing. The Nazirite vow is the most sacred vow my people can swear. It's a special dedication, and my dedication was supposed to last my entire life."

"So how did you break your vow?"

Samson lightly brushed the stubble on his scalp.

"I allowed my hair to be shaved."

The boy laughed, "That's it? You cut your hair and your god destroyed your life?"

Samson became enraged. He lunged toward the sound of the laughter, flailing his arms wildly in an attempt to reach the mocking boy. The chains around him tightened, and he fell to the hard dirt, spilling his grain all around him.

"If I hadn't broken my vow," he muttered, spitting dust and seeds from his bleeding mouth, "I'd still have my strength, and you'd be dead."

He could feel the lad's presence looming just over him, almost taunting him to try to attack.

"So this special vow allows you to kill people?"

the boy asked innocently.

Samson rose slowly, fumbled for his millstones, and grabbed another fistful of grain before the guards discovered him not working again. The monotony of the chore lulled the former champion into a quiet trance, and he found himself repeating the instructions of his vow that his mother had forced him to memorize as a child. A sudden thought dawned on Samson for the first time.

"Actually, one of the key parts of the vow was to avoid dead bodies of any kind."

"And you always kept that part?" the boy probed.

Visions of lions and foxes and wedding guests flooded Samson's mind. He could see their faces, almost as if seated in judgment of his past actions, recalling every infraction he had ever committed. The faces blurred to a swirl of hazy color, and coalesced into a terrifying image of Samson, heaving in exhaustion, bathed in blood, a jawbone in his trembling fist, surrounded by a sea of corpses.

"I broke it so many times," Samson cried, "and I never even knew it."

"What about wine and grapes," the boy continued, "did you always avoid them?"

Samson remembered his wedding, all the other parties, and every night with Delilah. He was more of a failure than he had ever imagined.

"And, of course, you kept all of the other laws — like not intermarrying with pagans, and not seeking revenge for yourself, and not committing adultery or murder, or dishonoring your parents."

Samson's entire body began to shake.

"You're an Israelite, too?"

The boy answered after a long pause, "I'm familiar with your laws."

Samson shook his head and lamented, "Shaving my hair wasn't when I broke my vow; I had broken every other part of it so many times. It was the last remnant, the only thing I had left. That's why God punished me. I had finally rejected everything."

"God's not punishing you," the boy said confidently.

"Obviously he's punishing me," Samson snapped back, "and he should! I deserve it!"

"If he wanted to punish you, why didn't he do it the first time you broke your vow?"

Samson had no answer for that. The more he considered the question, the less sense his entire life made. Why had he been allowed to defile everything: his vow, his life, his family, his culture, his religion? Had he ever been connected to God?

"Doesn't it seem a bit delusional to believe that your behavior dictates the behavior of an omnipotent being?" the boy asked. "You know, everything that happens to you is not a reflection on you, and everything that happens is not a reflection of divine wrath."

"But there are consequences," Samson insisted. "There are always consequences for poor choices."

"Not for you. Not for years, according to you."

"I guess God is patient," Samson speculated, "but eventually he snaps."

"Or there's more at play here than you can see or imagine."

Samson seethed, "I've spent my entire life at play in the hands of God. I had no say in any aspect of my life! I was named a Nazarite before I was born; I was named a deliverer before I was a boy; I was named a judge before I was a man. I never had a choice!"

After a long pause, the boy asked, "So your predicament is your god's fault?"

"No, no, it's my fault, but...."

"Why must there be blame?"

Samson shuddered in silence.

"You blame yourself for forsaking your vow, and you blame your god for forcing the vow upon you. How does all of that anger help you?"

Samson dropped his head in despair, wondering what sort of child this was to ask such probing questions.

"Maybe you are held in your god's hand, but not in wrath or manipulation, but in love. Maybe your discontent blinds you to that, and all you can see is your own misfortune."

Samson laughed to himself. He couldn't see anything, but the boy was right. Despite his blindness, Samson had refused to see anything other than his own unhappiness for a long time. And the longer the child talked, the more serene the former champion felt. An eerie peace slowly surrounded him, and he was almost smiling as his hands returned to grinding grain. A heavy footstep dropped next to him, followed by a kick that scattered his bowl of grain.

"Up, slave," the guard commanded.

Samson placed his hand against the cold, stone wall and rose to his feet. The chains that held him to the prison wall were loosened, and he felt himself being pulled out of the cell. He turned his head and called out in fear.

"Where are you taking me? What about the boy?"

Two guards laughed, "What are you talking about, you crazy, blind man?"

"I'm still here," the boy quietly assured him.

"Please don't leave me," Samson pleaded.

"I will be with to you even to the end of the world," the boy promised.

Samson was pulled along several corridors. Suddenly, he could hear the roar of an enormous crowd. Hissing and jeering surrounded him, and above him was an even louder noise. Only one structure in Gaza could house such a multitude. He was in the temple.

"The mighty Samson," an evil voice roared.

Thousands of voices joined in a deafening chant.

"Samson! Samson! Samson! Samson!"

Someone struck his face, and Samson collapsed onto the stone floor. The entire temple exploded with laughter.

"The scourge who ruined our land and murdered our citizens has been neutralized!"

More cheers as Samson was raised to his feet. He was slapped repeatedly.

"Who hit you?" they taunted. "Can you tell us, prophet?"

Samson staggered in darkness. His shoulder struck the curved surface of a massive pillar. He draped his tired arm around it. He just wanted all of this to be over.

"Dance for us, mighty man!"

Samson began to weep, imagining silent tears

streaming from empty sockets.

"Are you still with me, boy?" he asked.

"I'm still here."

Samson heaved, "Can you position me between the two largest pillars?"

There was no answer, but he felt a tiny hand pull his arm toward another column. Samson slumped against the cold facade. The riotous cackling of the crowd throbbed in his ears.

"Strengthen me one more time," he pleaded quietly, "so I can exact revenge for my two eyes."

Almost against all faith, Samson flexed his arms and began to push against the pillars. He felt tiny arms wrap snugly around his leg.

"Just let me die with the Philistines," he whispered.

The pillars shifted slightly amid the continuing roar of the hateful crowd. Samson's entire body trembled in exhaustion and trepidation and resolve. A slow and quiet rumble began to grow out of the darkness.

THE TRUTH OF GOD

A SLOW AND QUIET RUMBLE BEGAN TO GROW OUT OF THE DARKNESS. The black storm swirled overhead, and flashes of lightning danced between the thick folds of clouds. Job and his friends peered up at the strange mixture of darkness and light. Stiff winds began to blow around them, growing stronger and more violent, until the very dust from the ground pelted their skin like swarming locusts. Job fell to the ground and curled into a ball. The open sores on his body were torn apart in the tumult. He howled in pain and screamed in fear, but the terror did not relent.

As the storm strengthened, drowning all sound and light from the scene, Job felt his entire body sliding through the sand. The storm was pushing him like a clump of weeds, then turning him over, rolling him through the dirt until he was coated with dust. All he could see through his filmy eyes was brown. All he could taste was chalky death. He could no longer feel his own body, nor discern where his form ended and the dirt began. It was as if he had melted into the earth.

Then his whole being shot upward. He was thrust into the churning winds and clouds of the storm.

Spinning violently with all the debris of the land, he flailed helplessly, thrashing against the whirlwind as black darkness became darker. The sharp pricks of rocks and dust dissipated, and eventually he could feel his flesh again. When the tempest subsided, he found himself suspended in a void of absolute blackness, floating silently, feeling neither alive nor dead.

A blinding light exploded like a supernova all around him, and he heard a voice that sounded like a sonic boom.

"Who would try to dim my radiance with empty words? You try to explain the unknowable by clawing at things you can never understand. Brace yourself now, Job, for the real trial begins."

Through the burning beams that shone brighter than a thousand suns, Job could see swirls of dust and streams of color fusing and exploding as they hurtled through the void. The clouds collapsed into brilliant nebulas, where flashes of white light mixed with clumps of every color. Some disappeared into the distance; some seemed to hang over and around him. In time, he was surrounded by stars and galaxies, some familiar, some foreign. Bodies of rock and ice flew past him. A gaseous blob of red filaments began spinning before him, swirling faster, collecting pieces of energy from seemingly nowhere until it almost encompassed the entire space around him. Then it shrank in an instant as if a powerful speck in its center had sucked all material into itself. The red became orange, the orange became yellow, and the heat of a blazing sun hovered over him.

As he marveled at the sight, pieces of rocks began to cling to one another under his feet like flecks of iron drawn to a magnet. The chunks of rock grew, frequently pummeled by other stones, until Job found himself standing on solid ground. The rocks beneath his feet cracked, and jets of gas and water erupted all around him. The sky over his head filled with clouds and rain, and he was soon standing on a solitary mountain surrounded by a raging ocean. Winds blew from every direction, pressing the waves into intricate patterns and shapes, and soon a discernible shoreline appeared, glistening under the bright blue sky and a brilliant sun. Every type of flower and tree sprouted from the earth, and animals of every kind emerged from the new growth. The mountain shook violently, sending Job tumbling down the rocky cliffs until he finally crashed onto the beach.

"Surely you can explain everything you've just seen," the voice boomed again. "What's more, you undoubtedly possess the power to create and destroy everything around you. You are like a god in your knowledge and ability!"

Job opened his mouth to speak, but the ground began to tremble beneath his feet. The trees behind him shook, then collapsed under the weight of an enormous beast. It towered like a mountain above everything else, and its body looked like it was made of iron. A thick frill surrounded its massive head, and a giant horn protruded from its beaked mouth. It lifted its head and roared into the sky, and the sound of its voice made the ground shake like an earthquake. A tail longer than a river and thicker than a tree cut through the remaining vegetation, revealing four enormous legs that made an elephant's limbs look scrawny. Smoke rolled from the creature's nostrils, and it lowered its head to stare at Job.

The smallest whimper crept from Job's lips, and the beast charged. Trees parted like blades of grass before the creature's mass, and the entire land-scape shook with fury. Job staggered backward, his heels sinking into the shaking sand along the shore. The ocean waves seemed to grab at his feet, pin-ning him to the earth as the monster neared him. A roar erupted from its terrible mouth, sending a torrent of blistering wind that reeked of sulfur and death. There was nowhere Job could go. He braced himself to die.

The beast lowered its head and thrust its great horn at Job's body. The man flew like a tiny toy into the air and plunged into the sea. Stunned and momentarily suspended in floating silence, he eventually searched his body for wounds. Miracu-lously finding nothing, he swam to the surface and gasped for breath. Darkness had covered the en-tire area, and there was no sign of any land. Thick spears of lightning cut through the sky overhead, some of them piercing the waters around him.

The rise and fall of the waves became more pro-nounced, and the water began to bubble around him. Giant swells washed over him as an enormous, black form rose from the turbulent ocean. The snake-like neck of another monster twisted through the stormy clouds. A shrill scream cut through the thunder and roar of the waves. Lightning crackled over the surface of the creature's body. The beast was illuminated with ghastly sparks, turning its image into a metallic monstrosity.

Again the serpent screeched, baring repeating rows of glistening teeth. Job shuddered. A jet of flames burst from the monster's mouth, lighting the water itself that surrounded Job on fire. The searing heat scorched his face as he struggled to stay afloat. Thrashing among the waves, Job saw the beast's head dip below the flames. Giant spikes rose out of its back, and they began to circle Job as the serpent cut through the turbulent waters. Faster and faster the creature swam, spinning the flames around Job into a swirling glow of plasma. Within seconds, Job found himself in the middle of a violent whirlpool.

His body was helplessly pulled downward to the bottom of an inverted cone of twisting water and fire. Far above him, he could still see the black sky and the lightning. From that backdrop, he watched the dragon arch over the ridge of the whirlpool and descend upon him, its mouth gaping, its teeth bared, its breath aflame, its rage bellowing. Job lifted his hands to cover his eyes. He braced himself to die.

But the serpent plunged into the water inches from his face. The force of its weight thrust Job upward. A violent cyclone formed around him, and he was lifted into the sky in a giant waterspout. Lightning crashed around him and through him. Fire spun around him and through him. Terror flew around him and through him. Again he found himself flying through stars and clouds and nebulas of color he could never imagine or dream. As he rose through the heavens, the water and fire and lightning faded into a sparkling haze of colorful gems and swirling pigments. And from out of the strange, new environment, he heard a familiar, terrifying voice.

"Surely you can tell me all about my greatest creatures. Why you could probably even tame them, and turn them into your pets. There is no one on earth like you, one who can summon storms and control monsters!"

Job knew better than to try to speak. Within the fantastical haze of the cloudy realm he thought he could discern the form of a man approaching him. As the figure approached, Job realized the man was a giant. He began to tremble, wondering what terrifying being he was destined to encounter next. Emerging from the billows of brilliant color was a glowing figure with four wings that towered over Job. Without warning, Job felt his body drift upward toward the giant's face,

The closer he floated to the face, the brighter it seemed to shine. Job shielded his eyes, barely able to discern human features on the enormous head. The giant man said nothing; he simply stared at Job with expressionless eyes of fire. Then the giant turned his head to the right, and the blunt face of an ox-like creature appeared. Job gasped audibly. The ox had the same glowing face and eyes of fire. Again the giant rotated its head, revealing the hooked beak and feathered pattern of something like an eagle. One more turn, and Job found himself staring into the face of a fiery lion. Suddenly, the lion roared. Job screamed and fell backward into nothingness. At the feet of the giant, he could see more of its kind emerging from the colorful fog. The monstrous figures surrounded him and began to beat their wings furiously in unison. The action created a hurricane of wind that tossed Job like a leaf within the center of the throng. As the gusts grew more violent, Job was thrust upward in a twisting funnel of wind and light.

He soared higher into the heavens and strained to see if any monsters were pursuing him. A stream of red fire blazed past his face. Tossing about helplessly, he flailed his limbs, fighting to avoid more sinuous trails of flame. The shapes increased and swirled around him. Through the haze and the flames and the wind and the light, he thought he could discern long, thin, serpentine bodies. Blazingly hot, sharp tips scratched across his face. His body gradually stilled, and a hideous form appeared before him — a flaming snake with six fiery wings and a human face. Fire and smoke poured from its mouth, and its flowing hair kept switching between the appearance of dancing flames and writhing snakes. More dragon-like beings appeared and seemed to be speaking, but Job could hear nothing over the rushing din of wind and fire.

Thin tendrils slowly emerged from both sides of the monster's body, eventually becoming arms, eventually becoming hands. The beast grabbed Job, and the searing heat of its touch coursed through the man's body like a shudder of thunder. With an effortless toss, the creature thrust Job into the air, and again he was hurtling through the heavens. He flew for what seemed like hours, and eventually came to rest on a hard, cold surface.

Job took a moment to catch his breath and take in the scene. Clouds of every color still rolled around him. He pressed his palms against the surface beneath him. It appeared invisible, as if it were the clearest glass or crystal ever fashioned. Slowly rising to his feet, he noticed music that he could never hear before, a sound that almost seemed to have pervaded everything the entire time, like an eternal song. The sound came from every direction, but somehow seemed stronger in the distance before him. He began to walk, drawn to the enticing music. Brighter flashes of color and light formed ahead of him, and as he neared them he could make out the shape of a massive temple. It glistened and refracted in the hazy color, almost as if it were an illusion, but it also appeared to be the most real thing Job had ever seen.

Drawing nearer, he noticed a massive set of stairs that led up to the temple, with glowing angels ascending and descending. He lifted his foot to climb the stairs, but with every step, he seemed to remain on the flat, crystal path. He was ascending without ascending, moving but not moving, walking and yet flying. The floor was still firm beneath his feet, but somehow all sensation of movement changed as he passed through the towering angels on either side. The walls of the temple appeared and disappeared, and then he realized the entire structure was clear like the path. At times it appeared the temple was made of diamonds, then crystal, then cloud, then light. An evanescent aura surrounded him, again appearing real and unreal at the same time.

At some point he must have entered the temple because he found himself walking past columns of massive statues. As he passed, he shuddered, realizing the statues were alive, and they were the same four-faced monsters he had encountered earlier. They still glowed, they still fumed, and they still terrified, but they stood in reverence along the walls that led to a massive throne at the end of the room.

Above the throne, the winged serpents of fire hovered. They almost rested atop a glimmering green rainbow. Beneath the rainbow was a throne the size of a city. It gleamed as if adorned with every color of every precious stone, and many that Job had never seen before. Seated on the throne was an enormous figure that was barely discernible through the brilliant light emanating from its body. Job collapsed onto the floor and closed his eyes. Somehow the light from the being on the throne pierced his lids with the same intensity. Then the entire temple erupted.

The giants and the serpents began bellowing something deafening, and the entire structure shook with more violence than the strongest earthquake imaginable. Thunder crashed under the sounds of their voices. Job lifted his head to see lightning explode everywhere, enveloping his entire body in a web of electricity. Thick smoke billowed from massive fires that raged from the throne. Somewhere among the noise and the terror, Job could faintly make out the words of God that subtly ripped through his eardrums.

"Would you still dare to face a God you cannot survive with questions you cannot understand?"

Job could see, hear, and feel nothing and everything. He covered his head and softly whimpered, "Please, make it stop."

He felt a weight press upon his frame so strongly that he began to believe he was going to be crushed. His breath became shorter and sharper. The pain increased, but he refused to uncover his ears or open his eyes.

"I know now that I understand nothing," Job thought. "I spoke of things I thought I had heard, but now with all I've seen, I realize that I am simply dust and ashes. I'll never say another word."

He believed that he would never speak or even breathe again. It felt like he was being flattened against the floor. Suddenly, the pressure ceased, the noise quieted, and the light dimmed. He slowly opened his eyes to find himself lying in the dirt. Raising his head, he blinked his eyes repeatedly, squinting at the world around him. The hazy landscape slowly came into focus.

THE HAZY LANDSCAPE SLOWLY CAME INTO FOCUS. Adam rubbed his hand across his forehead. His skin felt hot and cold at the same time. Icy drops of water rolled down his arm. He had never felt anything like it before.

"Where are we?" a groggy voice groaned next to him.

She sounded different.

"I don't know, Eve," he answered.

He braced his hand against the ground and tried to sit up. A sharp pain pierced his palm. He howled and lifted his hand to his face. A small hole had been punched into his palm and a trickle of red liquid oozed from the wound. He stared at the odd marking for only a second when he realized his entire hand looked strangely drab. He glanced at his wife. The brilliant bronze glow that had colored her body was gone. All that remained was a dull brown hue.

"Where are we?" she pleaded more earnestly.

"I don't know," he snapped.

He pressed his palm against his lips and licked the burning spot. A strange, salty taste filled his mouth. The previously sweet scent of his flesh had vanished. He brushed his fingers through the grass. The turf was barely green, almost yellow, and the leaves were much more rough, almost like blades. He peered around the dense forest that surrounded them. Everything had changed.

"It's as if all the color was sucked out of the world," he mused quietly.

"Not just the color," his wife observed. "The very life of everything is gone."

Adam glanced fearfully at Eve and whispered, "He said we would die."

Eve began to tremble. Adam stood, and a strange aching seemed to rise from his bones, eventually emanating from his mouth in an audible groan.

"What was that?" Eve demanded.

"I don't know, but I can't move. My entire body feels so much heavier."

Eve struggled to stand as well, and yelped when her body brushed against the sharp leaves that hung listlessly from the surrounding trees. Adam shifted his weight uncomfortably and pressed against a briar of thorns.

"This is not Eden," Eve exclaimed.

"Wherever it is, we need some form of protection or this land will destroy us."

Adam grabbed the large, rough leaves of what looked like a former fig tree. The edges of the leaves cut into his delicate hands. He fought through the scorching pain, continuing to snatch more leaves and strands of gray vines which he rammed through the thick fibers of the leaves. After several grueling minutes, he tied the heavy garment around his torso like a piece of armor. Eve tried to do the same, slicing her own body in numerous places during the process. Once they were both covered, they tried to walk, but soon found their feet similarly punctured by sharp rocks and plants that covered the terrain. They borrowed the same leaves and vines to fashion crude sandals and resumed their slow trek through the woods.

They had no idea where they were going. Nothing looked familiar. It was as if they had fallen asleep and been transported to another world, an ugly, hostile, disfigured world where their own bodies had been perverted. Maybe this was their penalty for eating the fruit. Maybe this was death.

In time they emerged from the dark forest onto a craggy overlook covered with wild, thick growth. Adam and Eve slogged through the tangling weeds and muddy rocks until they reached the edge of the precipice. Peering down they discovered a familiar scene.

"The four rivers," Adam gasped.

Beneath them was a broad waterway that cut through a shallow valley and eventually split into four rivers. It was a unique configuration that held a special meaning for the couple. Gorgeous trees of every color had once lined both sides of the primary water source of their garden. Fish had darted through the crystal waters like a rainbow dancing within the streams. Hundreds of creatures had formerly filled the dazzling fields of multi-colored grass, drinking from the sweet waters and frolicking in the warm sun of a golden sky. Adam and Eve were standing in the very spot where they used to end every day after a long walk. It was once their favorite place in the whole world. Now everything had changed. Everything was gone.

"What happened to Eden?" Eve whimpered.

The river which had teemed with color and life now crawled like a wraith. White water wove through grayish, empty fields. The sky was blue and polluted with thick wisps of similarly white blobs, mirroring the same stagnant scene on the ground. Even the sun was a shadow of its former glory, and its rays actually felt cold. The whole world had faded, morphing into a hazy memory of what it should have been.

"Listen," Adam whispered.

"I don't hear anything," his wife answered.

"Exactly. The music is gone."

A sweet and constant melody used to fill the air around them. The voices of a thousand winged creatures fueled the song as they soared throughout the heavens. All of it had disappeared, replaced by the empty void of a breathless silence.

"We didn't do this," Adam finally said. "We couldn't do this. This was him."

He turned to look at Eve's tired, aged face. She shook her head.

"The serpent didn't have this kind of power."

"Not the serpent, God. He did this to punish us for what we did."

"But why would he punish the whole world?"

The ground beneath their feet trembled. Adam glanced at Eve. At least one thing hadn't changed. As dead as the earth had become, it still couldn't physically handle the footsteps of God. He was coming.

"I don't know, but I'm not waiting around to ask him," Adam blurted in a panic and dove back into the darkness of the wild wood.

Eve scrambled after him. The couple crouched among the thick thorns and weeds, hoping the pale foliage would obscure them from God's sight. They had never tried to hide from God before — they never had a reason to do so — but now, scratched and sore among a nest of unfamiliar plants that lacked any life and color, they began to fear that their attempt was ridiculously futile. That fear was confirmed within seconds by a thundering voice that nearly split their skulls. Adam covered his ears and clenched his head tightly. He glanced at Eve. She was in just as much torture. He remembered all the walks and talks they had enjoyed before to-day, never with any trepidation, never with any pain. No matter what they thought they could ac-complish by hiding, he was now certain they were about to be destroyed. Why had he never seen the sheer terror of God before?

Again the voice roared. Was God calling his name? He could recognize no discernible sound or word, just a violent noise that pierced every cell of his body. Despite the pain and confusion, Adam felt a force pulling him to his feet and out of the dark growth. He was terrified, but he was almost unconsciously approaching the source of his fear. A small part of him longed for the past and the way he used to feel when God would call. The ground continued to tremble with the colossal footsteps. Adam and Eve stood trembling in the gray path, staring at beams of light that radiated from the distance. Limbs and leaves drooped in the fiery light, some turning to ash before their eyes.

Once again the deafening sound filled their ears. This time Adam thought he heard a definite question — "Where are you?" — but not in his head. He swore he could feel the reverberations in his chest.

"I was hiding," the man cried to the burning air.

A blast of hot wind burst from the intensifying light. It melted the makeshift clothes the couple had fashioned, leaving them standing stark naked again in the middle of their condemned garden. Adam could feel the repeated prickling of a thousand needles over his flesh. Everything hurt, everything blinded, everything deafened, and everything horrified. He still couldn't hear anything but noise, but something kept nagging at his soul, pressing a continual question against his very bones until he could stand it no longer.

"Because I was afraid," he screamed.

The noise and fire continued to rage, filling his head with such pain that he thought it would explode. He could discern nothing from the experience, and none of it reminded him of his past encounters with God. Finally, he shrieked the question he had been longing to ask since he had awakened.

"Why is all of this so different? What happened?"

All at once the garden quieted and the light dimmed. Adam opened his eyes and could barely make out the hazy silhouette of a figure swimming in a foggy glow. He glanced at the trees to his right. They were still gray, but they were clear. Something was changing in God's appearance. A barely audible whisper drifted over Adam's ears.

"Did you eat from the forbidden tree?"

The man couldn't answer. He simply nodded.

"Then what is happening is what I promised. You're dying, along with everything else. You have cursed all of creation."

Warm tears began to stream down Adam's face. The blear only further obscured the form of God.

"But why punish everything for something we did?" Adam blubbered.

"I'm not punishing the world; I'm simply withdrawing from it. You have introduced the curse of sin, and sin cannot survive in my presence. So either I destroy the world by remaining who I am, which you experienced briefly when I first approached, or I destroy myself to save the world. I'm choosing to fade into oblivion so that the earth can continue to live."

"But it hardly looks alive," Eve observed.

Adam reached for his wife, realizing for the first time that she could hear the same thing.

"That's the result of my abandonment. It will continue to decay, as will you. But it's the only way to save you from absolute desolation."

The light was almost completely extinguished, nothing more than the image of a dull glow from a dirty sunset. Within seconds, Adam and Eve could no longer hear anything. God's voice was simply a thought in their heads, and his presence was indiscernible.

"We can't see or hear you. How will we find you now?"

"In time, you won't. And your children will struggle even more. That's why I told you not to eat the fruit. Now you know evil, and you will spend your life in sweat and tears trying to find me through all of that evil. And most of your descendants will fail."

Adam shook his head. "This isn't a world I want to live in."

"Believe me, the alternative is worse."

Adam wrapped his arms around Eve. Their embrace was cold, as lifeless as the world around them.

"And now you must go. There's a whole world out there for you, all of it more wild and terrible than this garden could ever be. But you've taken me out of this world and you've forfeited your home. Since you wanted knowledge for yourself, now you must forge your own life and shape your own world. It will be awful, and in time will only worsen, but someday, long after you're gone, I'll set it right. But it will be a long, painful, desperately evil ordeal until I can do so. You had me; now you have only suffering."

Adam and Eve held each other as they turned to go. They had no idea where they were headed; they had never set foot outside of the garden. But God was right. As they walked, the landscape became harsher and bleaker and more barren. Adam glanced back at the garden, but he couldn't see it. Eden was gone. He gazed up at the tired sun, wishing this was simply a dream from which he would soon awaken. A single beam of sunlight pierced his right eye.

A SINGLE BEAM OF SUNLIGHT PIERCED HIS RIGHT EYE. Elijah shook his head groggily, rubbed his eyes, then squinted into the morning sun streaming through the opening to the cave. He slowly sat up and held his breath. There was still no trembling earth, no blinding light, no burning fire, no visible God. Elijah hung his head and began to cry. The journey of four hundred miles combined with the desire of a thousand years mixed with the weight of a hundred thousand sacrifices collapsed onto the prophet like a soul-crushing avalanche of pain and despair. He watched his teardrops form vague shapes in the dusty ground, and thoughts of death returned to haunt his mind.

"What are you doing here, Elijah?" he sensed the Lord asking him, interrupting his brooding thoughts.

Elijah gazed around the cavern excitedly. He was still alone. It wasn't an audible voice; it was the same inner monologue that he had always heard, nothing more real than if he were imagining the dialogue.

"You know why I'm here," Elijah shouted at the walls.

"I do, but do you know why you're here?"

"I'm here for you," Elijah shrieked in desperation. "Everything I do is for you. My work, my words, my life — every waking moment is focused on you, and I am all alone. Your people ignore me in the same way they ignore you. They reject your statutes and refuse your sacrifices. They've destroyed your altars, they've defiled your name, they've destroyed every prophet you ever sent them, and now they're trying to kill me."

Elijah panted in exhaustion, somewhat amazed at his audacity and honesty in the moment. He waited a long time for any response. Nothing came until his breathing calmed and his heart rate slowed.

"All of that is true, but none of it is true, and none of it has anything to do with why you're here,"

Elijah fell to the cave floor in exasperation. He couldn't continue this peculiar dance with an unseeable and unreachable partner. He was done.

"I want you to say it out loud," God continued to prod. "I want you to ask for it."

"I told you what I want," Elijah groaned.

"Why are you here?" the silent voice persisted, burrowing deep into the prophet's brain until his head began to physically ache. "You intentionally ran for forty days and nights specifically to this spot. Why this place? Why this mountain?"

"Because I need to see you like Moses saw you," Elijah blurted almost unconsciously. "I need you to be physical; I need you to be tangible; I need you to be more real."

Another long pause was followed by a simple phrase.

"So you say."

Elijah lifted his face in the darkness of the cave, confused about what was going to happen next. What did that mean? Was he about to get his wish?

"Step into the light. I'm going to pass by and give you what you request."

Elijah's heart leaped in his chest. He jumped to his feet, but before he could take a step, a sudden onrush of wind assaulted the mountain and swirled inside the mouth of the cave. Rocks began to fall from the ceiling and walls as the wind quickly grew more violent. Elijah was tossed to the ground amid raining rocks and twisting winds. A deep crack opened in the ceiling just above the prophet, and worked its way toward the back of the cave and down the wall, splitting the stony sanctuary in two. Eventually the wind died just long enough for Elijah to note that the Lord was not in the wind.

Again Elijah tried to stand, but the ground beneath him began to tremble. The entire mountain convulsed with the rumblings of a great earthquake. More rocks littered the floor around the fallen prophet. The earthquake shook the whole landscape for several minutes. When it finally calmed, twelve large, polished stones were piled in the center of the cave. Elijah wondered at the odd arrangement for a second, but quickly realized the Lord was not in the earthquake.

Once more Elijah rose. He took one step toward the mouth of the cave when the air outside began to glow red. A powerful heat radiated from the opening and quickly filled the room. The prophet fell to his knees just as a billow of flame exploded into the cave over his head. He pressed his chin against the stone floor and listened to the roar of the inferno that raged both outside and inside. The fire burned hotter than anything he had ever experienced, but faded as quickly as it had flared. Elijah turned to look at the only remnant of the fire, burning atop the peculiar altar in the center of the cave. There was something mystical and inspiring about the fire, but the Lord was not in the fire.

The subsided fire left a silence that transformed the simple cave into a temple bathed in the soft glow of its altar. Elijah approached the altar and held his hand over the hallowed flames. The fire was not hot, but somehow kept burning. As he brushed his hand through the glowing flames, he thought he heard the faintest whisper. He paused, and then swore he heard it again. Pulling his cloak over his face, he exited the cave.

An otherworldly scene surrounded the mountain cave. Immediately it felt as if all sound had been absorbed into the towering rocks, leaving an oppressively heavy silence. Shimmering rainbows sparkled through the dry mist of a clear fog. Elijah squinted at the swirling colors, most of which he had never seen and could not possibly describe, mysteriously finding them both blindingly brilliant and softly subtle. Remnant stones from the previous storms littered the ground, but also floated around him. Elijah reached out to touch one of them in disbelief. The stone spun slowly while suspended in the air as if dangling from an invisible string.

Suddenly the prophet noticed the shadow of another man in front of him, strangely shrouded by the colorful streams of clouded drapery. For a moment he thought it might be his own reflection, but it became clear the stranger was moving independently, even though he made no sound and never became clear. Turning to the right, Elijah found the massive silhouette of a figure, large enough to be a second mountain sitting atop the mountain. The hulking form seemed to be facing away from Elijah, looking into the distance. Following the gaze of the giant, he noticed three more shadowy figures clustered just beyond the ridge. Elijah wondered if he was even on Mount Horeb anymore. Had he been transported to another land or another realm?

The familiar voice repeated, "What are you doing here, Elijah?"

"I told you, I wanted to see you. But right now, I don't know what I'm seeing."

"Why are you here?"

For the first time, the voice seemed to be audible. Elijah tilted his head and stared at the mountain figure, feeling like the voice was coming from it.

"I don't know what you want."

"I want the truth. I want your soul. Why are you here?"

"I alone have followed you," Elijah screamed at the shadow. "I'm the only one. Your people have rejected your laws, your priests have defiled your altars, your leaders have ignored your decrees, and your prophets have all been slaughtered. I'm the only one left who cares about you, and now they're trying to kill me. Everything that you created — from Abraham to Moses to me — is about to die."

Elijah struggled to catch his breath after the rant. Somehow he sensed, by only observing the hazy back of the dark giant, that the colossus was smiling.

"Finally we are speaking heart to heart."

The prophet gazed at the strange shapes and colors around him. He had so many questions, but no remaining strength or will to pose them. He, like the rocks, was helplessly suspended in silent awe.

"Every dream that you saw last night reflected a moment when everything I created could have died. In fact, that moment is eternally imminent. It is a fantastically fragile beauty I have formed. But I have sworn by myself to protect it. From the fall to the flood, from the slavery to the statutes, from the captivities to the cults — I have always saved a remnant, even if it was only one person, and it is very rarely ever one person, I have ensured a continuous lineage of my family. You need to believe that will never change."

"I try to believe," Elijah cried, "but sometimes these realities feel more real than your dreams."

"Then you need to see things as I see them. Look at the figure to your left, and you are looking into the past; look at the figures in front of you, and you are looking into the future. This mountain presently exists simultaneously in three distinct times. Beside you is your hero, Moses, experiencing a vision of my presence a thousand years ago. Before you are three men experiencing the same vision a thousand years from now. Yes, a thousand years from now there will still be people following and worshipping me. And here you are, believing in your tiny vision and imagination that you are alone, realizing that you are always part of a larger story and genealogy."

Elijah's heart leaped in his chest, and he took a step toward Moses.

"I can actually talk to Moses?"

"No," the mysterious voice almost laughed, "he's been dead for centuries. You can see a shadow of him, as if staring through a glass darkly, but this span of millennia, these three distinct times, can only exist in my mind."

Elijah pointed toward the three figures in the distance, asking, "And who are they, the ones who still follow in the future?"

"They are the ones who will expand Israel to encompass the whole world. Much of what you preach and hope for they will see fulfilled, and as much as you revere Moses, they will think even more highly of you."

"Can they see me now as I see them?"

"You are all experiencing this as one, despite being separated by millennia, and unable to interact with one another in any way. But just as you are inspired by Moses, those three men are inspired by you, and in truth, you are all inspiring each other in a glorious trinity."

Elijah still found it difficult to understand what he was seeing and hearing.

"After this you must return the way you came," the Lord continued. "I have chosen three people that you must seek out to anoint: Hazael will be king of Aram, Jehu will be king of Israel, and Elisha will be your successor. Yes, your time is coming to an end. But don't believe for one second your life has been in vain or that you are all alone. In addition to Elisha, I have over seven thousand true and faithful Israelites who have never worshipped an idol in any way."

The prophet collapsed facedown on the ground in reverent awe.

"Thank you for this. Thank you for everything," he spoke so quietly it was barely audible.

"Don't thank me yet. As you saw in your dreams, my appearances can be unsettling. Sometimes the thing you've wanted your entire life becomes the thing you never want again."

As the voice faded, Elijah could feel the rocky soil trembling beneath his hands. The atmosphere around him rapidly grew hotter and the wind began to swirl. The stones that floated in the air were sucked into the shadowy form before him, along with the dust and fire and fog. It seemed as if the air itself were fleeing, being forcibly drawn into the massive form, leaving a vacuum of silent emptiness. The form of God felt as though it was increasing in weight, and that weight was swallowing all of reality into itself. Sight, sound, scent, and smell — everything disappeared, and for a split second, Elijah looked up and thought he saw God's back.

Then a blinding supernova exploded, returning all the matter back to its place in the world, and the form of God ripped through the mountain and into eternity. The heat and weight of the moment were crushing, the rush of the wind was deafening, and Elijah screamed into the earth as his body was flattened into his soul. It was over in an instant, though it felt like it raged for hours.

And suddenly it was silent. Elijah lifted his face to find everything gone and everything returned. Gone were the misty colors and hazy figures and floating rocks. Returned were the drab, sandy, stone surfaces of Mount Horeb. In the aftermath, the prophet shakily rose to his feet and surveyed the area. Tears filled his eyes because he couldn't even remember where Moses and the others had been standing just moments before. It was as if the vision had never happened. But it had happened, he thought. It had to have happened because he was a different man. He closed his eyes and laughed to himself. As uncertain as he had been when he arrived on the mountain, he was now even more confident of his mission and position.

Like a giddy child he stumbled down the rocky crags of the mountain. When his feet hit the desert floor, Elijah ran. He ran with zest; he ran with zeal; he ran to serve his God. He ran into the red sun that hung over the sands of Damascus, repeating the names of the men he had been ordered to meet, and dreaming of the names of those he would never see. Despite the heat and the sweat and the burning air, he ran like a wild beast that could not be tamed, with the constant reminder of an ever-present God washing over him like a cooling fountain. With every step he felt his strength increase, with every breath he felt his life increase, and with every thought he felt his faith increase. The merciless sun beat hot on a cold man's heart.